Other Books
by Larry M. Greer

American Neanderthal

Does God Play Golf?

The Ghost of Keowee

Heaven is in Union County

Soft Target

Tomb Society

D1528900

Appalachian Trail After Dark

ISBN-13:
978-1544663968

ISBN-10:
154466396X

Cover Design by Rick Schroeppel,
Elm Street Design Studio

Dedication

This book is dedicated to Jacque Greer Bell who participated in a two week hike in the North Georgia Mountains with two of her cousins. That hike in 1972 inspired this book and the character Quenlyn McGuire.

This hike was Jacque's first backpacking adventure and she proved a very capable and enjoyable hiking companion.

To be clear, the violent and criminal scenes depicted in this story are purely fictional.

Appalachian Trail
After Dark

By Larry M. Greer

Chapter 1
Blood Mountain –
Thursday, February 15, 1973

Without opening my eyes, I knew it was going to be a miserable day. Rain danced on the rusty tin roof over my head and my feet were still sore from yesterday! In fact, my whole body was sore. I found the thought of putting on my cold soggy boots repulsive. When I finally gathered the strength to pull my head out of the warm sleeping bag, just enough to lean on my elbow and peer out of the Hog Pen Shelter, the only thing I could see through the dense fog, was an legion of grey trees stretching to infinity. It was going to be a miserably dreary day for hiking the AT. The only good part of getting up was the knowledge that I was leaving this broken-down lean-to of a shelter. Not one of the AT's better accommodations, in my book! The Hog Pen Shelter had actually been abandoned a number of years ago when the trail was rerouted and it certainly lived up to its name! Hanging a ground sheet above our heads during the night had been the only way to divert the rain that had been leaking through the sieve-like roof. There had been little talk among the three of us as we heated water for our hot chocolate and dined on energy bars. Today's hike south to the Blood Mountain Shelter would be a grueling 9.3 miles...with significant elevation changes...and weather challenges.

This section of the trail in north Georgia, was painfully absent of switch-backs. The rain quickly made it a precarious climb as we sloshed our way through red mud and over slippery roots and boulders. The two inexperienced hikers, sporting new boots, that had not been sufficiently broken-in and weatherproofed, were beginning to feel hot spots that would quickly become blisters. The tree roots, or trail snakes as I like to call them, were the worst. A seasoned hiker will focus on the trail rather than the scenery, so they don't end up face down on the ground. Not far into the hike, my wet socks were effectively accelerating the size and discomfort of my blisters. I did not want to stop in the rain to administer moleskin, but I realized that if I didn't take care of my feet now, I would pay dearly later, so I found an old Chestnut log that could serve as a convenient medical table for my wounded feet. I let the others continue ahead while I dug the moleskin from my pack.

By late afternoon, darkness was fast approaching and the temperature was already plummeting toward single digits. A little after four o'clock, we arrived at Neel's Gap. It had taken us all day to travel 6.9 miles and we still had 2.4 vertical miles left. For hikers used to the AT, 9.3 miles is not an unreasonable distance to cover in one day, but the frigid rain had accompanied us the entire hike, making the going slow and miserable. Thank God we'd had the foresight to fork out money for Gore-Tex rain suits. Even with that protection from the elements, I was beginning to realize that hiking with my two cousins Sam and Quenlyn in February had not been the best decision of my life. I guess you could call it 'hiker's remorse'.

As we descended the peak, the ancient Blood Mountain Store came into view and my saliva glands began to crave ice cream and maybe a couple of hot dogs. This rustic stone building stood beside Georgia State Highway19 and right on the Appalachian Trail. In fact, the trail ran right through the building. This haven for hikers was always a welcome sight. The store was crammed wall to wall with items backpackers needed after weeks on the trail. But, being February, the trail was almost void of hikers and so a sign on the door read 'Reopen March 1st'. March was the month that through-hikers heading for Maine started at Springer Mountain, the Southern terminus of the 2,200 mile AT.

Our disappointment at finding the store closed was palpable. The three of us plopped down on the bench outside the store and said nothing. Daylight was vanishing, being replaced by the foggy gloom of the night before. An occasional truck could be heard laboring its way up the gap, the sound of its engine reverberating off the mountainside. The trucks sped right past us without taking notice of the three figures in blue rain suits.

The last segment of the trail that we had traversed today had been mostly downhill. My feet repeatedly jammed against my new boots and were killing me. I decided that I needed to take clippers to my toenails tonight and add two Aleve to my dinner menu. The rain that had been with us all-day was now beginning to freeze on the branches overhead. I knew this meant that the weather at the Blood Mountain Shelter could be frigid and the 2.4 miles we had left to hike would be icy.

The old bench nestled under the store's extended roof, sheltered us form the deteriorating weather. You could hear it hitting the leaves on the ground and watch it bouncing off the pavement. The longer we sat there in our damp clothes, delaying the uphill climb, the colder we felt. The chill factor now had to be well below freezing.

Reluctantly, after finishing off my water and a box of raisins, I got up. We all hefted our wet packs onto our backs and with no words exchanged, we crossed Hwy 19 to begin our ascent up Blood Mountain. In my mind, 2.4 miles to the top was not a bad hike, but according to the trail guide this particular 2.4 miles was rated 'difficult'. The trail was now becoming a real challenge as the sleet intensified. The two hiking poles had also been a good investment. They had saved me from landing on my ass more than once that day.

In 1934 when the AT trailblazers laid out the path heading north, the concept of switchbacks must not have entered their minds. Those who have hiked this part of the trail in Georgia know there are many places where the trail goes straight up a mountainside and then straight back down, burning every muscle in their body.

Among the three cousins, at 40, I was the one most out of shape. Sam had told us that after a few days of hiking, we would be in excellent shape. Well that was debatable! As we trudged up the trail, I decided we should consider staying over a second night at the Blood Mountain Shelter. We had planned to have at least one lay-over day for rest. Right then, I was hoping for two. My body ached from head to toe and I felt like a saturated sponge. Like many other hikers, I wondered, "Why in the Hell I'm doing this to myself, and in middle of the winter to boot."

About one mile into the ascent, the rain and sleet were turning into snow, creating an entirely new challenge. Over decades of use, many parts of the trail had experienced significant erosion, creating waist-deep trenches. So, as darkness and snow drifts impacted our ability to see undulations in the trail, our progress slowed even more. Efforts to breath negated our ability to talk, so we slogged on in silence. All we wanted was to make it to the shelter so we could discard our cold wet clothing and build a fire.

After two miserable hours, we arrived at the summit. A couple of dark boulders loomed before us in the twilight. At first they blocked our view of the shelter. As we rounded the corner, despite its advanced state of dilapidation, we were delighted to see it. One corner of the roof was beginning to cave-in and it was obvious that the structure should have either been repaired or torn down years before. Despite our relief at having arrived, not one of us moved to cross the entrance. Snowfall increased, giving this scene an eerie atmosphere. Ominous, could best describe our impression of where we were about to spend the night.

The stone structure had been built back near the time the trail had been developed and was constructed out of the plentiful supply of nearby rock. It was nothing like the three-sided shelters on the rest of the trail. This shelter did not even have a chain link gate. The entrance was wide open to the elements and any four-legged creatures that might want to join us. I was the first to venture across the threshold. I could see that the windows at one time had shutters, but had long since rotted away and the windows sported only a few shards of broken glass. The wind and snow was free to swirl in and join us as well.

Unusual among AT shelters, the dirt floor was littered with paper and remains of other hikers, making me wish I had the option of a tent tonight. Once fully inside, we could see that the structure contained two small rooms which were divided by a stub wall. A fireplace sat in the middle of one room. This raised my hopes for a nice fire, but no one had been thoughtful enough to leave dry wood from which to build a fire. As in most shelters, there were small notes left by hikers tucked in the wall crevices.

Curiosity caused us to pluck out a few. One told about a place to get food further up the trail, but the one that really caught my eye read: 'Skunk lives here.' This warning, found in many shelters, never failed to unnerve hikers.

We dropped our packs and began to make ourselves as comfortable as possible for the night. We lit several candles, and I spread out my ground sheet and unrolled my sleeping bag. Even with the ground sheet between me and the dirt floor it didn't prevent me from feeling grimy in this place. However my stomach took precedence and the idea of a hot, nourishing meal was foremost on my mind. One by one, we lit up our gas stoves and began to heat hot water for soup and hot chocolate. In a shelter, the sound of a gas stove being lit creates an ear-piercing "sheeesing" sound. Tonight in this environment, the sound seemed deafening. The soup was just what I needed...hot and quick. However, I was so exhausted that I decided to pass on the mac and cheese I'd been salivating about on the trail. I had perched on a rock, thoughtfully rolled in by some hiker in the past and surveyed the surroundings. I thought I caught the whiff of some sweet-smelling meat. It seemed to be stronger when I faced the fireplace, so curiosity got the best of me and I donned my head lamp and headed toward the fireplace. Now I could see a small spiral of smoke rising from still smoldering ashes. The aroma was not all that offensive, but I didn't think we'd want to smell it all night long, so I poked at the ashes in an attempt to extinguish the smoldering coals. That didn't work. Now, despite my fatigue, I was on a mission so I stuck my arm and my empty soup cup into the snow just at the entrance to the shelter and scooped enough snow to put out the coals. That only made the smoke more intense and the smell stronger. Now my cousins began to complain about the odor, so I escalated my efforts using my handy pooper scooper. Finally the smoke dissipated, so to be entirely sure the fire was out, I took a stick and stirred the remains. This action dredged up one end of what looked like a big bone. O.K., now I'm wide awake. My curiosity piqued, I continued stirring the ashes until the object was completely exposed. It appeared to me that someone had killed and devoured a large animal, as it still had some charred meat on one end. Gingerly, I reached into the fire with my kerchief and pulled out the object. It was about 12 inches long and I thought that was unusual for a meat bone.

"Hey guys, come take a look at this. I found a really big bone in the fireplace and it seems someone had a barbeque."

Quenlyn groaned, "Oh please don't make me get up to look at your bone. For God sake, can't you see I'm already in my sleeping bag and I'm dead tired?

"All right then lazy bones just lay there and I will bring it over there for you to examine."

"Hawk, don't you have anything better to do?"

I picked up the end that did not have the charred meat on it and took it over to Quenlyn. She rose up on one elbow to examine the bone. With her head lamp shedding light on the bone, she looked at it closely, turning it end over end. Gingerly she handed it back and said.

"Wow! I don't think this is just any bone!!"

"What do you mean?" I asked.

"Well, I'm no expert and only a nurse, not a doctor, but this doesn't look like an animal bone to me. Since we are spending the night in this creeped-out shelter, I really hope I'm wrong, but it looks like a humerus bone."

"You mean like your funny bone." Sam chuckled from his sleeping bag.

"No you idiot, I mean like the upper arm bone of a human."

"Well." Sam said, still finding this somewhat funny, "Let's don't get too carried away. I mean, there are all kinds of animal bones. Back in school I worked part time in a supermarket meat department and I saw all kinds of bones that size."

She held the charred meat end of the bone out toward me. "This is freaky! Have either of you ever had grilled meat or barbeque that smelled like this? Now I'm even more spooked by what I thought I saw today. I could feel someone behind us, but every time I turned around, there was no one there."

In an attempt to calm Quenlyn down, I added, "OK, I agree with Sam, let's don't get too carried away. Try not to let your imagination go wild. Get some sleep and we'll look at it in the light tomorrow morning. Maybe we can hang around for an extra day and get some down time. By then maybe the weather will be better and we can continue our hike for Springer Mountain."

They both agreed, as the urgency for sleep outweighed their curiosity ab out the bone. Once they were snug in their down sleeping bags, the night became very still. The snow silenced many of the normal night noises of the forest. Only the conversation of a couple of hoot owls interrupted the stillness. The snow would continue into the night and occasionally gust in through the broken window panes. Quenlyn knew from previous nights in the shelters, that the sound of small scampering feet were mice looking for crumbs or warm places to sleep. She shuttered at that thought, as two nights before, an adventurous mouse discovered that her long blond hair was a comfortable place to curl up and had gotten himself tangled in her curls. This resulted in a screaming fit. Who's to say whether she was more frightened or the slumbering mouse.

Tonight she lay there trying to sleep, but that bizarre experience today was lingering in her mind. She just knew there had been someone behind them, but neither of the guys saw anything and as for that, neither had she. But she sensed a presence following them just out of site in the fog. In the wee hours of the night, sleep finely overcame her exhausted body and weary brain.

Sometime around one a.m. I woke needing to reliever myself. It was still snowing and I guess by now, it was at least a foot deep. The shelter was close to a rock outcrop and in the dark one needed to be careful. As I was standing there taking care of business, out of the snowy darkness rose a blood curdling scream. It reverberated from the valley below, sounding like someone in great agony. Then two more times the scream echoed up the mountain side. This put cold chills through my body and I dove back into to the shelter, running head-long into Sam, who, having heard the scream, was bolting out of the shelter.

Chapter 2
The Three Cousins

Samuel Hardgrave, at the age of 41 was a very good looking man. His thick dark hair was stylishly cut and he always dressed in the latest styles. His shirts and trousers were freshly pressed with precise creases. Sam, just over 6 feet tall, caught the eye of every girl and was the envy of his peers. He was a graduate of the prestigious Citadel Military College in Charleston, South Carolina and had entered the Air Force as a Captain. When his military service was completed, Sam knew he wanted to teach, so he headed to Mississippi State University completing his Ph.D. in education. He was delighted when a small Southern university offered him a teaching position. He quickly rose to be President of the University. It was not long before his management and people skills were noticed in Washington and he was offered a prominent position with a Federal agency. By the time he was 41, he had made the 'Who's Who in America' list in five separate categories.

****

Quenlyn Maguire was born in 1949 into one the South's most successful manufacturing families. She had inherited her father's type-A personality, and nose for business. These traits fostered success for both father and daughter.

Quenlyn had the benefit of attending a top notch private finishing school and at the age of 25, she had become a very sophisticated young woman. What you first noticed about her was her long strawberry blond locks and her sweet Southern accent. She excelled in her father's business but her passion had always been nursing.

One of the other things her father taught her was a sense of adventure. And this trip down the AT with her two cousins was proving to be just that. As she lay in her sleeping bag at the Blood Mountain Shelter, unable to sleep, she thought back on a similar adventure hitch hiking in Mexico with a girlfriend.

****

Hawk Maguire was born in 1936. He was a product of a blue-collar mill family, prevalent in the South in the early 1900's. With four brothers and sisters, an opportunity to attend college was out of the question. School had not been easy for Hawk but he was a hard worker. Not having the luxury of a car as a teenager, he was delighted to land a job driving a city bus. Quenlyn's father noticed his work ethic and offered him an opportunity to work in his textile company. He rose quickly in his uncle's firm and adapted the same sense of adventure. The willingness to take calculated risks served him well in business and fueled his curiosity about the wilderness. However, he had begun to wonder if this February hiking trek had been a wise decision.

Chapter 3
Christmas 1972

As they did every year, the Maguire family gathered for a traditional Christmas at Jack Maguire's spacious home. This year was no different than most, with at least 100 family and friends welcomed and well fed. The festivities included Jack's favorite songs, performed by one grandchild or another and a plethora of the same stories repeated to everyone's delight. The aroma of oyster stew wafted through the air and everyone knew this would be the first of many courses. With a family this large, cousins were in abundance and they tended to gather in small clusters based on their general age groups. Samuel Hargrave was generally considered the leader of the 30-40 age-group and his cluster of cousins reveled in hearing tales of his adventures each year. So when I overheard Sam weaving a tale about hiking in the Smoky Mountains, my ears perked. Without thinking, I interrupted Sam's tale. "Oh, that is something I have always wanted to do."

With a wicked smile across his face, Sam offered, "Well Hawk, I'm thinkin' about a winter hike, say in February?"

"Wouldn't that be rather cold in the mountains that time of year? It's December and it is cold as Hell right here."

"Oh, it'll be cold alright! But that is why I'm going in February."

Now a chorus of 30-40 something cousins chimed in simultaneously, "Why?"

Loving that he had everyone's attention, Sam continued, "Cause I have been on any number of hikes over the years. Most of them were in warm weather. So I want to do a winter hike."

"Do you mean this February, like in 4 weeks?", I said incredulously

"Yup. My plan is to leave about the middle of the month and hike for maybe two weeks." Sam grinned and said, "Why don't you go with me?"

"Well, I guess I could take off work, but I'm really not in shape for the mountains. How do you get in shape for a trip like that?"

"You can start now by walking hills around here, but at your age, you could probably start out the hike and in about three days, you'll be as fit as I am."

"You're kidding me, I mean look at me. I'm forty years old and feel like a chicken dumpling."

Quenlyn, who had been listening to this exchange walked over and said, "You two are crazy. You'll freeze your butts off up there in February."

I decided to taunt my favorite cousin, "Bet you couldn't do it! If you weren't such a scaredy-cat, you could go with us. After all you just graduated from nursing school and don't have a job yet."

"Are you serious? You want me to tag along?"

Sam laughed, giving Hawk a sidelong glance. "I bet you could beat him up those hills and most likely me as well."

Quenlyn giggled and responded. "I don't know about that. And besides, I don't have a clue what kind of stuff I would need to hike in that winter environment."

"If you two are game to do something really adventuresome, go with me on this hike. You can come to Atlanta next week and I'll take you to my favorite backpacking store and get you outfitted."

"Hey Sam," I added, "How long is this hike you are talking about?"

"According to the trail guide, it is approximately eighty-six miles. Hawk, it's not a long hike, but it gives enough time to lay over during the trip to rest up."

I was really beginning to get excited about doing this two week trip with my cousins. What stories I'd have to tell back at work. "Let me check at work and I'll call you in a couple of days. I'm really getting stoked about this possibility. What about you Quenlyn?"

"Hawk you're right, I don't have a nursing job yet so if you and Sam don't mind, count me in."

Chapter 4
North Georgia

Just off the Appalachian Trail between the Blood Mountain Shelter and the Woods Hole shelter, 1.2 miles to the south, is a tiny spring. It is the only available water on this part of the trail. Regular hikers know this spring and are willing to risk the hundred yard scramble down a steep embankment to reach the precious water. Because there is no water at the Blood Mountain or the Woods Hole Shelter this little spring becomes lifeblood for hikers.

The icy cold water from the spring tumbles over moss cover rocks where it joins another small stream. It is at this point that it takes on the name Slaughter Creek. Here, a logging road to the right is marked Slaughter Gap Road and eventually becomes Wolf Pen Road which runs into the town of Suches in Union County, Georgia.

Slaughter Creek tumbles its way to the foot of Blood Mountain through heavy thickets of Rhododendron and Mountain Laurel. Any hiker on Slaughter Road intent on scrambling down the bank to the small stream would have no knowledge of the old log cabin hidden behind the foliage. The crude structure had been built in the late eighteen hundreds and was safely nestled in a thicket beyond the creek. Old growth Rhododendron had reached such a height that the cabin was nearly invisible. From the outside, the cabin appeared small. Its rusty tin roof apparently had leaks, as someone had placed a black tarp over one side. There was a small window on the front and one on the back, covered with tattered curtains, aged by the sun. Two 55 gallon drums rested against the side wall next to the chimney. The door was the only part of that structure that looked sturdy. A handmade sign, written in red, warned 'Keep Out'. Other than this sign, it appeared the cabin was unoccupied. Nothing littered the ground around the house and no smoke rose from the chimney. However, a path was warn from the cabin door to an outhouse about two hundred feet below west end of the cabin and well away from the creek. If anyone investigated, they would find that the cabin sat on a large track of wilderness owned by a logging company that had abandoned its mill some years prior. Power was not provided up Slaughter Creek Road; therefore the cabin had no electricity. It was so secluded that no one knew of its existence or its occupancy.

But someone did live in that little cabin. Johnny Greene was a hermit by anyone's definition.

Twice a month, out of necessity, Johnny took the bicycle he kept inside the cabin and pushed it up the hill, out to the road. He varied the path he took to the road, not wanting to create a visible trail leading directly to his cabin. Maintaining privacy was very important to Johnny. Once on Slaughter Gap Road he pedaled his bike five miles into the tiny community of Suches, Georgia. Here he would fill his backpack and two saddle bags with the supplies needed to sustain him for two weeks.

Johnny's routine was to head to the hardware store first, then the grocery store and finally to drop by the post office to see if there was any general delivery mail for him. He evaded people in general and avoided being pulled into any conversation. Suches was nestled in a high valley on the western side of the AT. Most people knew their neighbors, but Johnny was known only as an 'odd ball'. Some speculated that he ran moonshine, but he never appeared to have any to sell. And he never purchased large quantities of corn or sugar, both necessary ingredients for corn liquor. He did buy bullets for his rifle and shells for his shotgun and when questioned, he just said that he loved to hunt squirrels.

The most unusual thing people noticed about Johnny was that three times a year he would order two five gallon cans of formaldehyde from the hardware store. This had to be special ordered so Johnny would pay cash up front. When Amos Smith the proprietor inquired about Johnny's purchase, he was told that Johnny liked to stuff animals. A number of the locals who were avid hunters were also into taxidermy, so Amos thought that was a reasonable answer. When Johnny's formaldehyde order arrived, he would pay one of the local residents for the use of an old pickup truck. He would drive the buckets and his groceries to the edge of Slaughter Gap Road and haul them to his cabin. He would then return the truck and ride his bike back home.

During warm weather, he always wore the same clothes. This consisted of a pair of thread-bare bib overalls and a tee shirt that one time was probably white. Now it had taken on a sweat-stained color. He was missing two front teeth. The remaining front teeth would occasionally peek through his unruly facial hair when he talked. His hairy arms were tan and muscled. His hands appeared oversized and that brought attention to his jagged dirty fingernails. Johnny Greene never smiled and never looked anyone in the eye. Every time Johnny ventured into Suches and was forced to communicate, saliva from his chewing tobacco would leak from the corner of his mouth. People were disgusted by this sight and when Johnny observed their reaction, he would wipe his beard against his shoulder. That did not have the effect of changing people's reaction to Johnny's appearance.

Johnny always paid in cash and in a small community, people were curious about where he got his money. Joe McNeill the postmaster would only say that once a month Greene got a small package from LaGrange. He had no clue what was in the package, but it always came from the same return address with no name.

One morning on Johnny's monthly visit, he made his way into the hardware store and asked Amos, the proprietor, for a box of 32 caliber bullets and a Bowie knife.

Amos unlocked the glass case that held the knife display and Johnny pointed to the largest one in the case, which sported a ten-inch blade.

"Sounds like you are goin' deer hunting Johnny."

"Yea, goner kilt me a buck I be seeing up in the woods."

"Well, when you shoot em, you gonnna have the right knife to skin and gut em with."

"Yea, Need 'bout 36 feet of dat rope too."

"Sure you want 36 feet?" Amos asked, "That's a lot of rope for hangin' a deer in a tree."

"I said I wanted 36 feet. Lots I need it fer."

Greene put his hardware purchases in his pack, with his groceries, straddled his bike and headed for home.

The minute the bicycle was out of sight, Joe McNeill walked out of his post office across the street to the hardware store. "That sucker is the weirdest guy I ever seen." What'd he get from you this time?"

Amos replied, "Oh this time it was stuff for deer huntin'. Knife, bullets and rope and the like. You know, Johnny always has a wad of cash so I'm glad to see him, but each time he comes in, he frightens me a little.

****

Christmas 1972 came and went in the Suches Valley. Not much happened during winter months in the high mountain town. On Tuesday February 13th, Greene made his first trip of the year into Suches. It had been a little longer since his last visit so he'd need more supplies this time. His routine didn't vary, however. After leaving the hardware store, he would buy the groceries he needed and head to the Post Office. Joe watched him as Johnny headed his direction to pick up the package from LaGrange. Each month, Johnny would leave the Post Office and walk to the abandoned store down the block. There he would open his mail. Whatever it was in the package, he would stuff in the pocket of his bib overalls and toss the empty package in the trash.

It had become a regular practice as soon as Johnny left town, that either Joe and Amos would venture from their businesses and walk across the street to chat about Johnny's latest visit to town.

"Well Amos, what did old Johnny buy today?"

"Said he was short on kerosene and bought two gallons. He also bought some of those heavy duty razor blades like you use for scraping paint off walls. Says he uses them for skinnin' the animals he stuffs."

"Amos, did you ever hear anybody around here say that Johnny was stuffing a fish or some other animal for 'em?"

"Nope, come to think about it, never have."

"Joe, did you see all that black stuff on his overalls today?"

"I did indeed."

"I asked him about it, but all he'd say was that he got too close to a deer he gutted and got blood on him."

"Damn," Joe wondered out loud. "Think he ever takes a bath or washes his clothes?"

"Well, he don't stink real bad, but I got to admit" Amos said, "I seen a lot of hunters get blood on 'em, but not like that. It was all over him, includin' his cap and boots."

Chapter 5
The Trailhead

Quenlyn and Hawk drove to Sam's home in Atlanta on Friday February 2nd. Sam had a live-in girlfriend who was not into cooking, so Sam treated them all to dinner at his favorite restaurant in downtown Atlanta. He had invited them to spend the night and the plan was to hit the big outdoor store early on Saturday morning. When they checked out, Hawk, commented that this better be a really great ten day vacation because he had just spent over eight hundred dollars. Sam assured them that it was an up-front cost and their next hiking trip would only cost them their food.

"Yea," Hawk chuckled, "If there is another trip!"

A week later, on Friday February 9th, Quenlyn and Hawk traveled back down to Atlanta to pack up their new gear. They would head out early the next day for the Standing Indian Shelter on the AT trail that would become their starting point. Crystal, Sam's girlfriend would drive them to the trail and pick them up near the end of that segment of the trail at Springer Mountain on Sunday February 25th sixteen days later. The trip to Springer was 86.3

miles plus an additional few miles down a blue trail to an Inn where Crystal would pick them up.

Although Hawk and Quenlyn had walked in their new boots the week prior to their trip, they would come to find that this had not sufficiently prepared their most important piece of equipment. Sam had emphasized how important it was to break in the boots, but stopped short of complete instructions. He had also strongly advised they buy boot wax, but neglected to tell Hawk and Quenlyn this coating needed to be repeated several times for adequate water proofing.

Neither Hawk nor Quenlyn had ever eaten dehydrated foods before and she commented on how delicious it looked on the package cover. Sam just smiled at the clerk and said nothing. Were they in for a surprise!

Conversation was lively on the trip to the trailhead. Hawk and Quenlyn were wild with anticipation. It was a sunny morning with no clouds in the cold winter skies. Sam had been to Standing Indian Mountain before and he knew about a fire road used by rangers that would take them right up to the top of the mountain and eliminate any hiking that day. When they arrived around three thirty, it was 42 degrees and dropping rapidly. Sleeping in a shelter was a whole new experience for both Quenlyn and Hawk. When they began to unpack and blow air into the air pads Quenlyn decided she wanted to sleep between the two men. That suited us guys just fine. Both felt protective of her and knew this trip was not one her father had been fond of. Sam thought this was a good time to introduce them to trail grub so he made dehydrated spaghetti. It might not have been the best choice of meals, as all three were doubled over with gastric pain within an hour. Of course, none of them mentioned it to the others. "So much for the photos on the package," Sam thought.

Chapter 6
JC Cargill

John Cargill was born in 1946 and spent his entire childhood in the mountains of North Georgia where his family farmed 214 acres on the north side of Woody Lake near the small settlement of Suches. 'JC,' as he was called, had been a good boy. He helped on the farm during the summer and took responsibility for milking their few cows, throughout the year. He was an average looking man with blue eyes and rusty colored hair. His five foot ten inch frame was a mass of muscles for all the farm work. He didn't mind the farm work but his real love was the forest that surrounded the little mountain valley. Most any time he wasn't working, you could find him hunting and fishing in the nearby woods. It was obvious to his family that becoming a park ranger was his fervent desire, so they encouraged this interest.

There was a special training school for park rangers in Harpers Ferry, Va. JC drove to visit the school and before leaving, he applied for enrollment that Fall. Upon admission, he would also have to commit to 650 hours of study which included law-enforcement training. It took only 30 days before JC was accepted into the school. Georgia was where he had applied to work after graduation, so he also attended a special ranger training within the state of Georgia. By the time he had completed his training, two years had passed.

Jobs with the National Park Service were highly coveted and JC had to wait nearly a year for a position to open, but the available position, was his dream job. He would be responsible for 29 miles of the Appalachian Trail. It was the section between Springer Mountain and Blood Mountain. The salary would not be big, but that did not bother JC. He would be working in his beloved Mountains.

Chapter 7
Athens Georgia

Bob Chandler, at 21, was a third year student at Georgia Tec. He loved the outdoors and on most summer weekends you could find him hiking with friends. However when school started, he carried a heavy credit load, so finding a weekend to hike in the mountains was rare.

This February, in 1973, Bob had five days between the end of his winter semester and beginning a full load of classes in the spring semester. This was the perfect time to strike out alone for a little longer hike. His friends were good for about 2 days and his girlfriend could handle one night sleeping on the ground. So, this hike would be a good three days. He would begin his hike on Saturday, February 10th. A friend had agreed to drive him to Amicalola Falls where he would hike up a five mile blue trail that would put him at the top of Springer Mountain later that day. There he planned to spend his first night at the Springer Mountain Shelter. On Sunday, he would cover 15.8 mile to Gooch Mountain Shelter. The third day, he would hike 15.9 miles and end up at Neel's gap on Monday, February 12th. He planned to travel as light as possible with warm clothes and a sleeping bag and wearing light running shoes. Common sense told him to pack a rain suit as well. His pack would weigh in at eighteen pounds. Robert's total mileage from Springer to Neel's Gap would be 31.7 miles where his friend would pick him up late in the afternoon on Monday February 12th at the old Blood Mountain Store.

Bob was an experienced hiker and as rugged as the trail up to Blood Mountain was, with his light pack, he could make good time up that steep path.

On Monday, February 12, as planned, Joe Wheeler sat on a bench beside the Blood Mountain Store. At four-thirty, he had been waiting for two hours. The winds were increasing and the temperature was dropping fast in the late afternoon. Wheeler was growing a little anxious as he waited for his friend Bob to descend the trail and appear at the edge of the road. By nine that night, he had moved back into his car in the parking lot. Although he knew Bob could handle himself even in bad weather, he was very concerned. Bob was extremely punctual. He decided he would find a motel in Helen, just down the road. He would head back up to Neel's Gap early the next morning to see if Bob was there waiting for him.

Wheeler, a hiker himself, speculated that any number of things could have kept Bob from completing his hike at the planned time and none of his thoughts were good. When he arrived back at the store on Tuesday 13th at 8:30am, Bob was not waiting. By noon, Joe was alarmed. He had several conversations with a local plumber who was making repairs to the store while it was closed. He pointed out a poster on the wall near the front door that gave the Ranger's phone number at Vogel State Park. Just as Joe was about to make the call, a hiker came down from the trail. Joe grilled him extensively, but he had not seen any other hiker on the trail for several days. "Not many hikers in this cold weather. Lots of snow up on top of Blood Mountain." That was all the information Joe got out of the man.

At this point Joe called the Ranger Station and reported his friend missing. Bob was now almost a full day late. The ranger took all the information Joe could provide including Joe's contact information. They asked him to wait until dark but to call them back before he left Neel's Gap.

At four o'clock, Joe made a collect call from the pay phone to Bob's parents. Bob was always prepared and had provided Joe phone numbers in case of an emergency. Bob's father was alarmed and asked if Joe would stay over another night at the motel. He promised to cover both nights of Joe's motel bill and agreed to meet him early the next morning at the motel.

On Tuesday February 13th Ranger Paul Johnson called two separate county sheriffs and informed them of the missing hiker. They agreed to make contact with the ranger that covered that section of the trail.

Chapter 8
Sheriff's Office
Wednesday, February 14th

From her desk, Anne called out to Sheriff Dill. "The Ranger's office is on the line, Sheriff."

"What do they want?"

"I don't have a clue." Anne, hollered back. With a cup of coffee in one hand and a cigarette in the other, she transferred the call to the Sheriff's line.

"This is Sheriff Joe Dill, can I help you."

"Sheriff, this is Ranger Paul Johnson at Vogel State Park. We have a missing AT hiker that might be in your county. We just got a report late yesterday from our Amicalola office that a young man is reported to have left Springer Mountain three days ago and is overdue by a day and a half at Neel's Gap. The description we have is that he is a twenty-one year old on break from Georgia Tech. His name is Robert Chandler...goes by Bob. He is six foot tall with black hair. At this time we don't have a photo of him, but as soon as we get one, we will send it to you just in case he walks off the trail in your area."

"As I recall Paul, there have been two others in the past couple of years that were reported missing up in that area and they were never found."

"That's right Sheriff. We do have a ranger that works that section, but he is off today and out of contact. We checked with his family and they said he had taken his radio with him. So far he hasn't responded. The friend that was supposed to pick him up indicated he was prepared for the weather, but it's been in the low twenties every night for over a week up there."

Chapter 9
Blood Mountain, February 15th .

The three cousins had been on the trail for five days when they arrived at the Blood Mountain shelter. It was Thursday, February 15Th. The events of the evening and the condition of the shelter made for a restless night. It was one A.M. when Hawk had heard the blood-curdling scream.

"Sam, Quenlyn!!"

Sam had heard the sound too and was already headed toward the entrance, running head-long into Hawk.

Quenlyn heard the panic in Hawk's voice.

"I was just outside near the boulders and I very clearly heard screams coming from the valley below."

"You know it could have been an animal. They sometimes sound like screams, especially in the night," offered Sam.

"No, it was human. I'm positive!"

"What should we do?" asks Quenlyn.

"To tell you the truth, I don't know."

Again, trying to be the voice of reason, Sam suggested, "If the screams were way in the distance, we couldn't do anything anyway. Let's see if we can get a little shuteye and after day light we'll head to Woods Hole Shelter and see if it was coming from down there. It's only a little over a mile to the shelter and we could see if anyone needs help. It will be important for us to get some sleep and stay warm and dry if we're going to hike in this weather tomorrow."

Sam's advice seemed sound, so everyone piled back into their warm sleeping bags, but for some time, no one fell back to sleep. Dawn came both too early and too late, given the night's experiences. The snow was fairly deep and they would have to 'post hole'. The trail that was almost invisible under the blanket of white. However, with such an early start, they made it to the Woods Hole shelter by 7:30 am. It was positioned slightly off the trail and facing east to catch the morning sun. However, this morning it would not make any difference which way it was facing. The air was grey with fog as they approached the front of the three-sided shelter.

Sam was about a hundred feet in front of the other two and peeked into the shelter before

41

entering. He stepped back and warned, "Hawk, this may very well be where the screaming came from."

"What do you mean?" Quenlyn asked.

"See for yourself. Nobody goes off in this weather and leaves their sleeping bag and all their gear!"

Hawk surveyed the shelter. "If you ask me, I think there's has been a struggle here. The way things are scattered around isn't normal. Not even for a slob."

"Oh my God!" Quenlyn gasped. "Look at this." Beside the sleeping bag, lay a rather large puddle of what appeared to be blood.

"Shit" Hawk blurted. "I hope what happened here, isn't what it looks like."

Looking to their leader, Sam, Quenlyn inquired. "Well, Sam, what do we do now?"

Sam's thoughts were exactly the same as Quenlyn's question. What exactly did they do now?

"I'm not sure it's the right thing to do, but since I am more accustomed to these trails, I think I will take some water and a few energy bars and head back for Neel's Gap. There was a phone booth near the store and I think the best thing to do is to call the Ranger Station and report what we've seen here. I should be back here late this afternoon. You two stay put!"

Begrudgingly, Hawk and Quenlyn agreed. Neither one felt entirely safe without Sam, the experienced hiker. But they knew what had to be done. So, Sam headed back over Blood Mountain toward Neel's gap.

Chapter 10
Johnny Greene

Johnny's personality disorders could be traced back to his childhood. He was born in 1915, just before the great depression. His family lived in extreme poverty near a small community in north Georgia called Centerville.

They lived in a four room rented house in the country near a dairy farm. The dogs and chickens lived under the house to survive the hot summer days. A hand-dug well near the back porch supplied water and a path led to an outhouse at the other end of the property. No grass grew in the red clay yard that became sticky mud during the rainy season. The Greene's did have electricity, but it was limited to one naked light bulb hanging from a twisted cord from the center of each room. In the summer, Johnny's father, Moe would move the stove onto the back porch because the heat from the kerosene burners made the house unbearable. There was no fireplace to warm the small house in the winter, but a small cast iron coal-burning heater warmed the main room. In order for Ella May to wash clothes she would build a fire under a large black kettle in the backyard and boil the clothes. Johnny and his older sister Elsey would wear the same clothes for a week at a time. Johnny had one pair of Bib Overalls and Elsey two printed dresses that her mother had made for her out of fifty pound Dixie Darling flour bags. Neither one of them owned summer shoes, nor was Johnny provided underwear. They told him it was because he would be cooler in the summer without them. Moe worked at a saw mill down the road. They did not have a car, so Moe would walk to work. Each payday, Ella May would walk to the small grocery store about a half mile down their dirt road. Moe gave her ten dollars and she would carry an empty feed bag to bring back the necessities she could not grow in her garden.

The majority of Moe's paycheck went for liquor. Sometimes he brought home moonshine in a quart mason jar and other times it was Old Forester bourbon. He would sit on the front porch and drink until he passed out. Ella May did the best she could with what was available and she didn't not dare ask Moe for more than ten dollars a week.

Moe was not a good father and worse, he was a mean drunk. Johnny knew that he needed to stay out of his father's reach, especially when he was drinking. If Moe even thought that Johnny was misbehaving, he would grab a leather strap he kept hanging by the front door and beat Johnny unmercifully. Even as young as five, he would try not to cry out in pain. This only served to make Moe angrier. Little Elsey would hang close to her mother during these beatings, because she did not want to be next.

In the fall of 1921 when Johnny turned six, he joined Elsey on the school bus. It was good to get away from the house. The old wooden-sided bus would stop on the road near their house and he would ride with Elsey to the Centerville School. The school's ten rooms served grades one through eleven.

Johnny's classroom had eighteen children and taught grades one through three. In the center of the room stood a mid-size black coal stove connected to a pipe that ran straight up through the ceiling. The windows were tall and on warm spring months were left open in hope of catching a breeze. Miss Black, a young woman of 28, was their teacher.

Behind the school a field of red Georgia clay served as their playground and at the back edge of that field sat two out-houses mounted up on a bank. When the wind blew just right, playing on the playground was a stinky experience.

Johnny's mother had never taught him the alphabet or his numbers. She could not read or write herself. So when he entered school for the first time, he was already behind his classmates. He was frightened every time Miss Black would head his direction to ask about a paper he was supposed to be working on or see if he needed help. Because of his father's behavior, Johnny was terrified of any person in authority. When Miss Black stood over him and looked down at his work and ask if he needed help, he would stare at the desk and answer 'No Mam'.

At recess, other boys made fun of him for wearing the same Bib Overalls to school every day. His shirts were thin and faded. When the kids figured out he would not fight back, it was common for one of the bigger boys to ruff him up while the others including, little girls would egg it on. Sometimes the teacher would break it up, but that only made things worse. Johnny was like a wounded chicken that the other chickens would chase around and peck at.

By the time he was twelve years old, he hated school. He hated the other kids including the girls. He spent a lot of his time thinking about how he could get out of school and out from under his father's authority. But nothing seemed possible. He had no money, and had never been out of Troup County. Over the next two years a couple of things changed in his life. Living in the county next to a dairy farm, he became intrigued with the bleached bones of cows and pigs he found in pastures. He especially became infatuated with skulls. He would bring them home and store them under his bed. One day he brought home a cow's head that was still in the final stages of decay. There was a small stand of pine trees close to the house and that was where he took his trophy. The maggots consuming the remaining meat captivated his attention as they crawled in and out of the eye sockets and mouth and ear cavities. He took his small pocket knife and cut off a small piece of the remaining flesh to see how rotten it had become. The brain cavity was of interest as well. He took one of his mother's large spoons and tried to dig out the liquefying brain matter.

One day, he found a dog that had been hit by a car not far from the house. After dark, he slipped out of the house and dragged the dead carcass to the pine thicket. The next afternoon, after school, he took his knife and a small hatchet to the thicket. Black horse flies swarmed, attempting to lay their eggs in the putrefying remains. This entire process of death and putrefaction fascinated Johnny. He cut the dog's stomach open and pulled the guts out for examination. Then he cut the legs off with his hatchet and cleaned the flesh and tendons away from the bone. Once he had completed this task, he cut the head off and hung it up in a tree to rot over the next couple of months. He wanted to put the dog's skull in a box and keep it under his bed along with two cow skulls. Even though most young boys are naturally curious about such things, Johnny's fascination was not even close to being normal. The dark side of Johnny's personality was increasing with each passing month. One sunny Easter morning, the neighbors' children down the road were given three lively baby ducks dyed pink for their Easter baskets. After the children had finished playing with them, Johnny noticed that the ducks were put in a tool shed for protection at night. The following Sunday while the family was at an all-day revival service, Johnny headed to the tool shed.

What he did next was a pivotal point that shaped the rest of his life. After making sure no one was around he snuck inside the shed. The late afternoon sun seeped between the boards giving him just enough light. He spotted the ducklings in a cage at the end of a work bench. Behind the workbench, hung an orderly array of hand tools. Along the back of the work bench, mason jars full of nails, nuts and bolts stood ready for a project. He removed the hammer from its place on the wall and laid it on the work bench. Then he lifted one of the three ducklings from its cage. By this time the little ducks were used to being handled and chirped in anticipation of being fed. But that was not what Johnny had in mind. He held the tiny head of one of the ducks against the work beach. In his other hand he picked up a ten penny nail, transferred it to his left hand. With two fingers, he held the nail above the ducks head and then with a well guided aim, slammed the nail through the duckling's head pinning it to work beach. The little pink duckling died upon impact. He waited to assess how he felt. There was a slight electric sensation that traveled up his spine, but nothing else, so he repeated this treatment on the other two little ducks.

The next morning the little girls were heading to the bus stop. They knew they had a few minutes before the bus arrived and simultaneously changed direction running towards the tool shed to check on their ducklings. The screams and cries brought their mother running from the house. When she saw the butchery, she felt a plethora of emotions...anger that someone could do such an act of violence, sadness for her daughters, and fear that whoever perpetrated this horrible deed might still be close by. She gathered the girls close to her, waved the bus on and headed to the house. Once the girls had been calmed down she called her husband, who in turn immediately called the sheriff and headed home.

The local sheriff was as repulsed by the sight of the three little ducks nailed to the workbench, as the family had been. He had no proof, but his first thought was the little Greene boy who lived down the road a piece. The father was known as a drunk and the teachers had complained about Johnny's behavior numerous times. The sheriff could not think of anyone else in the farming community except Johnny Greene that might have done something like this. Late that afternoon when he knew Moe would just be coming home from work, the Sheriff went to the Greene's house. First he talked to Moe privately, telling him of the incident the night before. Moe also immediately suspected his son. Johnny was called over to the two men, knowing that he was the first person they thought of for the duck mutilation. This sent seething anger through his gut, but unless he wanted a public whipping in front of the sheriff from his father, he had to hold his anger in. Of course when they questioned him about the incident, he denied any knowledge of what had happened to the ducks. He thought he had been convincing, but he could tell that neither his father nor the Sheriff believed him...only adding to his anger. The Sheriff's car was not even out of sight when Moe grabbed Johnny and began to shake him. To protect himself from the abuse that he knew was coming he shut down and was like a rag doll. His father continued to yell obscenities, shake him and throw him up against the side of the house.

"Don't lie to me boy, you little shit!! Don't think for a minute that I don't know about those dead animals yo been cutting on down in the woods. Yo done it. I know you did!"

With tears in his eyes he said, "No Pa, I never done it."

"Well I got good reason to believe you did, boy and I got a good notion to beat the living Hell out of you."

When Moe turned to grab the leather belt off the wall, Johnny knew it was now or never. He'd had a growth spurt this year and now stood five foot six inches tall and weighed 110 pounds. His father had not had a chance to start drinking when the Sheriff arrived, so Johnny knew he would take the full brunt force of his father's beating. So he whirled out of Moe's grasp and dashed off the porch and running hell-bent for leather across the field and into the woods. Fear and anger fueled his adrenalin. He knew his father was as familiar with these woods as he, so Johnny took circuitous routes and backtracked to see if anyone was following him. At twilight he realized he was very close to Jay Goddard's house, several miles down the road from his home. He spotted Jay near the barn. He slowed his pace, giving himself time to catch his breath and appear as if this visit was casual. He knew Jay from school. Jay was 16 and Johnny would soon be 14. Jay was tall for his age and thin. His blond hair covered his ears which was unusual for the time and an indication that, like Johnny, Jay was a bit of a rebel.

"Hey Johnny" Jay said. As much as Johnny tried to disguise his emotion, Jay could see fear and panic through Johnny's attempt at calm. "Anything wrong," Jay queried. Johnny hesitated, but Jay's attempt at friendliness caused Johnny to lose the mask and he blurted,

"My Pa's beat me for the last time and I ain't goin' back home. He's a drunk bastard and he beats me for no reason; I think just 'cause he likes it!" Johnny did not mention the ducks.

"Well what you gonna do?" Jay asked curiously.

"I don't readily know, but I sho ain't goin' back. No how!"

"D'you run all the way here?" Jay asked. When Johnny nodded, Jay continued, "So where you goin' next?"

"Dun know, but could I sleep in your hay barn ta'nite?"

At 16 Jay had no interest in girls, but was fascinated by the guys in his class. This might be an easy opportunity to get to know Johnny a little better. So he agreed.

"Sure Johnny. I'll sneak you something to eat and bring it to you after we finish our supper. I'll stay with you for a while and we can visit. There are a couple of old horse blankets in the loft and you could use them to make up a bed."

Johnny was surprised by Jay's eagerness to make him welcome, but was relieved to have a warm, dry place to hide. "You won't tell your Pa or Ma will you?"

"Hell no!", Jay retorted. "I got my own problems with my folks."

About an hour after dark, Jay returned to the barn and climbed up the loft ladder. He had a flashlight and a couple of jelly sandwiches along with a quart jar of sweet tea. He stayed and watched while Johnny ate. They talked for about an hour. Finally Jay laid his hand on Johnny's knee, "I got to head back to the house 'afore my folks come a lookin'". He told Johnny he'd return early in the morning before school and bring breakfast. He also cautioned Johnny to stay put in the barn for the day and he would be safe.

It was a chilly late October night, and although he felt warm and relatively safe, Johnny knew eventually his father would come looking for him. He couldn't stay there more than tomorrow and was not about to go home. He lay for hours trying to figure out what to do next.

In the morning he woke to the sound of voices near the house. He peeked through the cracks in the barns wall and saw the Sheriff's car and four people. He couldn't make out what they were saying, but he suspected the Sheriff was looking for him. He could see Jay being questioned and shaking his head in response. Finally the Sherriff got back into his car, rolled down his window and said something to Jay's dad. Then he drove off, slowly down the road, surveying the surrounding farmland and forest as he drove. Once the car was out of sight, Johnny relaxed just a little. It was two days in a row that the Sheriff had been down this road and Johnny Greene was the subject of the Sheriff's visit both times. Johnny knew that he had to make a decision and head somewhere else tonight.

He did not see Jay again until well after dark. He came bearing gifts of food and drink again. Johnny felt such gratitude toward Jay for helping him, that he decided he must finally have a friend.

"Sorry I didn't get you any breakfast this morning. Not sure if you saw the Sheriff, but he was askin' all sorts of questions and I was scared I might accidently look towards the barn, so I steered clear. You musta done somethin' real bad for the Sheriff to be so interested in findin' you. But I ain't gonna ask, cause we're friends." He patted Johnny's knee again, which ran shivers up Johnny's arms. He told Jay,

"I've had all day to think about what I'm going to do. But I ain't come up with anythin' yet."

"Johnny," Jay interrupted. "I'll let you in on somethin' I been thinkin' 'bout for over a year."

"What," Johnny asked interested.

"I want to get away from here and head to Florida," Jay blurted.

"Why'd you do that? I mean you ain't in no trouble are ya?"

"No, I'm not in trouble with the law, like I think you are, but my Pa's startin' to accuse me of things. He's tryin' to make me see a doctor in Atlanta so as he can change me and make me more manly, know what I mean?"

Johnny, knew what fathers could do to their sons and felt a little sorry for Jay. He must have looked puzzled.

"You ever heard the word 'queer', Johnny?"

"No," Johnny responded, not sure if Jay had changed subjects or continuing to talk about Jay's father's accusations.

"Let me 'splain it this way...do you like girls?" Johnny was thrown for a loop by this one.

"I can't say I do or don't. Never gave 'em much thought. Only girl I know is my sister."

"So you have never had the urge to get a girl down?

"Nope, never have. Heard other boys talk about it, but not something that interests me. So what does that have to do with bein' a 'queer'?"

"Well," Jay hesitated for a few minutes then appeared to make up his mind. "I just like guys better than girls. Know where I'm goin'?" Johnny wasn't sure and wasn't sure he wanted to continue this conversation. Jay however, had gotten a very warm feeling from explaining his sexual preferences to Johnny.

Chapter 11
Back to Neel's Gap

Sam left Hawk and Quenlyn at the Woods Hole Shelter and made record time hiking back the four miles up Blood Mountain and down to Neel's Gap. There were four cars in the parking lot, but no one was around. He suspected it was day hikers that had gone north on the trail where there was less snow. Two phone booths were located just below the Blood Mountain Store. As he was about to dial information to get the Ranger Station number, he spotted the poster taped to the inside of the next phone booth. It read: "in case of emergency on the Appalachian Trail, call" and it had the number for the local ranger station. He dialed the number on the poster and after three rings someone answered.

"Hello, this is Ranger Paul Johnson."

"Sir, this is Sam Hardgrave. I'm up at Neel's Gap. I'd like to report some unusual things my cousins and I experienced on Blood Mountain last night and today."

"What did you find, Mr. Hardgrave?"

59

"Well, early this morning around one a.m., we were at the Blood Mountain Shelter when we heard what sounded like a human scream. We heard it several times. I'll admit, we were a little spooked, so we rose early and made it to the Woods Hole Shelter by seven thirty this morning. We thought we maybe could help whoever was in trouble. What we found at Woods Hole was a sleeping bag, a pack and a lot of hiking gear, but no hiker. We figured no one would go off and leave all that stuff."

"Well, we see a lot of unusual things up here Mr. Hardgrave. He might just be on a short day hike," Johnson offered.

"Well," Sam continued, "that's not all. It looked as though there had been a struggle and food was sitting out as if the hiker had been ready to prepare his meal. But our greatest concern was a large puddle of what looked dried blood near the sleeping bag. We were afraid something really bad happened to the hiker, so I came down to the Blood Mountain Store and called you."

"That's certainly not good. I can see why you were concerned. Mr. Hardgrave, would you wait there at the store and I'll drive up and get you. It won't take long for me to get there."

"Sure, but I'm hoping to get back to my friends before dark. They are waiting for me at the Woods Hole Shelter."

"Sure. I understand. I can help you get back by way of a fire road that connects with the Slaughter Creek road. It has a side trail that leads up to the Woods Hole Shelter. I would not recommend that you and your cousins stay at the Woods Hole Shelter tonight...for two reasons. It could be that there has been some major trouble up there and we don't want to chance your group being endangered. We also don't need you to disturbing any evidence."

Ranger Johnson hopped into his truck and headed up Hwy 19 to pick up Sam Hardgrave. It was just after two o'clock when his radio crackled. It was JC Cargill.

"Hey Paul, sorry I didn't respond to your radio call, but I was off yesterday and neglected to turn my radio on. What can I do for you?"

"Well, JC things are a little more complicated now than yesterday. It appears we have two issues. First, we have a missing hiker that was supposed to have gone through your section earlier this week. He was headed for Neel's Gap from Springer and never arrived. He is now two days late. And second, not sure if this is related, but just got a report that it looks like some foul play up at the Woods Hole Shelter. Some hikers found a bag, pack and a puddle of dried blood, but no one around. Can you meet me at the trailhead off Slaughter Creek Road in about an hour?"

"Yes Sir, I'll be there waiting for you."

Chapter 12
Florida

In 1928, fourteen year old Johnny Greene and sixteen year old Jay Goddard left Jay's farm outside of LaGrange, Georgia and became freight car hobos. They caught a freight train outside of LaGrange that was headed for Atlanta. When they hopped into the dark boxcar they had no idea where it was headed, except AWAY from LaGrange and both their troubles. The plan was to eventually get into a boxcar that would take them to Lakeland, Florida.

They were excited to have made it this far without being caught. They headed to the back side of the boxcar in the shadows and settled down. It didn't take long for their eyes to adjust and discover that they were not the only trespassers. By this time the train was rolling slowly down the track and gaining speed rapidly. They talked quietly, gauging that the other hitchhiker sitting in the opposite corner, was an older man. They sensed more than saw that he was staring directly at them from under the brim of his hat.

The train's wheels against the rails made a significant racket as it sped through the night towards the city of Atlanta. Not wanting to be overheard, Jay leaned close to Johnny and whispered as loud as he dared.

"How much money do ya have?"

"Thirty cents."

"Thirty cents!! You serious?"

Johnny whispered back, "That's all I have. There was no way for me to ever have any money o' my own. Mom gave me a nickel every week for candy an' I saved it."

"Do you have any idea how far Florida is? I mean how far do you think thirty cents is going to get you?"

"I don't know. But I will find a way to get there. How much do you have?"

"Four dollars and eighty two cents," answered Jay proudly. That seemed like a fortune to Johnny. The only money he had ever seen was the ten dollar bill his father gave his mother each week for groceries.

Jay was quite for a moment then whispered. "You need to put that money in your shoe."

"Why?"

"Cause that hobo lookin' at us is probably thinkin' about robbing us."

Jay had packed some food and a jar of water for each of them and put it in a horse feed bag the night they stole away. Jay had also cut a steel water pipe into two pieces and handed one to Johnny. He said that was for protection on their trip.

As the freight train rolled on, it made a number of stops along the way. They noticed the hobo drinking something from a pint bottle, and figured it to be moonshine. Throughout the journey, they kept an eye on the old man and vice versa. As dawn peeked over the horizon, it brought a dip in the temperature and drizzly rain that periodically gushed into the boxcar's open door with the wind. It had been a long night. The boys did not realize how far away Atlanta was from LaGrange. As they noticed the changing landscape from farmland to a few houses and businesses, they hoped the Atlanta stop would be next. The boxcar did not offer much protection from the elements and both boys were cold and hungry.

The hobo had not said a word, just stared. As the train slowed again, he rose in a wobbly fashion, indicating that he might be a little drunk. He headed in their direction. It didn't take but a few wobbly steps for him to be looming over them with a toothless, malicious grin. "Say boys, you look like you could spare some money and I need some. So let's fork it over. Ya see, I'm 'bout outa my moonshine?"

Jay looked up at him and responded politely. "Sir, we don't have any and are heading for the Salvation Army when we get to Atlanta." Jay was wearing a coat over his bib overalls and did not look the part of a typical hobo.

"Come on fancy boy, I node you got some cash. You wan' ta give it ta me or ya wan' me to kick the shit out of both o' ya and jus' take it from ya?"

Jay felt paralyzed and couldn't think of a way to answer. He glanced at Johnny then down at his burlap bag. Instantly, Johnny knew what Jay was trying to convey and he prepared himself for what was coming. Slowly he slipped his hand into the horse feed bag. Seeing no compliance from the boys, the old man leaned over as if he was going to grab Jay for a beating. Johnny knew what that fear felt like, but he was surprised when Jay reached up and grabbed the old man's bib overalls by the straps and pulled the hobo down on top of himself. A struggle ensured. The old man, despite his age, was stronger and had begun punching Jay in the face. Seeing this, Johnny sprang into action to protect his new friend. He reached around in the bag and wrapped his hand around the lead pipe. Automatically, he sprang to his feet behind the hobo. Jay was holding off the hobo to the best of his ability but was quickly losing the battle. With a strength he did not know he possessed, Johnny whipped back his arms and swung down the lead pipe with everything he had. Not only was his blow powerful, but his aim was accurate. The pipe landed on the back of the hobo's skull and a crack could be heard even over the wheels of the train. Blood came shooting from his head and splattered everywhere. The hobo collapsed inert on top of Jay. After a moment, Jay was able to shove the man off his chest and breathe again. He said nothing to Johnny but just stared, wide eyed. Then he glanced over at the hobo and back at Johnny.

"I think you killed him!" was all he could think to say.

"Wasn't that what I was supposed to do?"

"Not sure, but I think ya saved my life," jay responded with a mixture of fear and relief in his voice.

"What do we do with him now? If someone should find us in this car, I'd don't want to have to explain how he died. 'Sides, we have blood all over us."

The train was still rolling at its normal pace. Jay leaned out the door and looked both directions. At this point there was nothing along the track but fields and woods.

"Let's push him out the door while there is time."

Jay, now having regained his composer, suggested they check the old man's pockets before they rolled him out of the car. They found two dollars and eight cents.

Jay shoved the money at Johnny. "Here, you keep it. T'was you who killed him and 'sides, you need the money."

The old man bounced down a steep bank and into a swamp. The two boys sat back down on the floor in silence. Now they could never go back home. Florida was not an option any longer, but a destiny.

Johnny just leaned up against the wall of the box car. He didn't understand it, but sensed an arousing tingle in his privates. It was as if he had just masturbated. He was baffled by his reaction to the violence, but he did like the satisfaction that he felt race through his body. It made him think of the animal parts back home. Now he wished he had thought to cut off at least a finger of the old man as a trophy.

Chapter 13
Slaughter Creek

In the early 1700's the Cherokee Indians moved into the lands occupied by the Creek Nation, south of the Smoky Mountains. The Cherokee desired the lands for themselves and history tells of a particularly blood battle in an area now known as Slaughter Gap. Cherokee tales tell of streams that ran red with blood. The mountain on the south side of Slaughter Gap is what we know as Blood Mountain, as a result of this significant battle. Was the ancient bloody battle a foretelling of what was occurring in February of 1973?

When Ranger Johnson arrived at the trailhead of Slaughter Creek, JC Cargill was waiting for him. Johnson introduced Hardgrave and explained what Sam and his two cousins had heard the night before and had subsequently discovered at the Woods Hole Shelter this morning. The sun would set just after 6pm and darkness was rising from the ground up through the trees where they stood. They could not afford to waste any time.

Ranger Johnson was impressed with Sam. He appeared educated and well-spoken. When Sam mentioned the meaty bone they found in the Blood

Mountain fireplace, Johnson visibly became concerned.

"Why do you think it was a human bone?"

"One of my cousins just graduated from the MUSC School of Nursing. She was almost certain that it was the upper arm humerus bone."

"What did you do with the bone?" Johnson inquired, concerned that they might have contaminated evidence in what was beginning to look like a very big problem.

"We handled it only with my kerchief, so hopefully we did not contaminate anything you might need. After examining it, I reburied it in the ashes to one side of the fireplace." Johnson's first impression of Sam was being reinforced.

"That is good. We will need to check on it in the morning."

The Slaughter Creek side trail up to the Woods Hole Shelter was steep. It was not well traveled and in places brushes had overgrown the trail and recent storms had dropped trees across it. The snow also hindered their pace. It was a difficult hike, even without backpacks. After an hour they intersected the AT where they headed south a few hundred yards before taking another shortcut trail to the shelter on the right. There was light smoke in the winter air as they made the approach to the shelter. Sam let out one of his customary loud whistles to alert the other two that he was near.

Hawk was sitting outside the shelter on a log poking at a fire he had built to keep his feet and hands warm.

Sam introduced Hawk to Rangers Johnson and Cargill. Then he looked around for Quenlyn.

"Hey, where's Quenlyn?"

Hawk looked surprised. "I thought she'd be with you."

"Why would you think that?" Sam said with a frown on his face.

Hawk then filled Sam in on the accounts of the day at Woods Hole Shelter. "Well, the sun came out and she was bored. You know Quenlyn. So she thought she would walk back up towards Blood Mountain to meet you coming back down the trail."

"How long ago did she leave?" asked Sam, now worried for his cousin's safety, having a better understanding of the dangers they might be facing in these mountains.

"I didn't look at my watch, but it must have been about two hours ago."

"Crap," exclaimed Sam. "I didn't hike back across Blood Mountain. I rode with Ranger Johnson around the mountain to a side trail that comes up here. It's gonna be dark real soon. I hope she is on her way back. Did she take anything with her?"

"Just a bottle of water, as far as I know."

"She took a coat, right?"

"Yes."

Rangers Johnson and Cargill had stepped away from the cousins to discuss Quenlyn further.

When Johnson saw the large dried blood stain on the shelter floor, he knew there was a serious problem.

"I think what we are looking at a crime scene here, Paul." Cargill confirmed.

"Let's get dispatch to contact Sheriff Dill and have him get up here tonight. In the meantime we need to make sure no one tampers with any of this."

Sam and Hawk had joined the two rangers near the shelter entrance. Johnson asked Hawk if everything was the way they had found it this morning.

"Yes sir! The only thing we did was to pick up a corner of the sleeping bag. That was when we noticed the dried blood and decided we needed to get ahold of you'all.

As usual, Sam was thinking ahead. "Ranger Johnson, it's almost dark and we don't have tent with us. Any suggestions?"

"It might be a good idea for you and Hawk to hike back up to the Blood Mountain Shelter for the night. You'll probably find your friend along the way."

Johnson hesitated, and then continued. "Is it unusual for your cousin Quenlyn to wander off like this? Have you told me everything?"

That question reminded Hawk of Quenlyn's suspicions on the trail. "She mentioned yesterday,

74

that she felt someone stalking us. She said on several occasions when she would look back, certain that she saw a figure behind us in the fog, but she never actually saw anyone. Sam and I didn't have the same experience, so we kind of blew her off."

Ranger Johnson was becoming increasingly concerned, but he did want Sam or Hawk to be alarmed.

The questions for both the Park Rangers and the Sheriff were mounting. First had been the report of the missing hiker, now two days late. Then the missing hiker at Woods Hole and now possibly even one of the three cousins had gone missing. Only forensics could answer whose blood was on the shelter floor, and that could take days...so many questions and not a clue to connect the incidents.

Sam and Hawk took Ranger Johnson's suggestion. They grabbed Quenlyn's backpack and headed the one-and-a-half miles back up Blood Mountain, with only the moonlight to illuminate the trail. Not surprisingly for February, when the sun disappeared, the temperature plummeted. The exertion of the hike would stave off the chill of the night, but it wouldn't stop their concern about

Quenlyn's whereabouts. Something was very wrong and they both knew it.

Chapter – 14
Florida - 1947

The remainder of Jay's and Johnny's hitchhiking trip to Florida had been without incident. They hopped off the boxcar for the final time in Lakeland, Florida. Johnny and Jay had easily found work in the orange groves in the spring of 1929. When the orange groves had no work, like the migrant Mexican workers, they moved on to sugar cane fields. It was hard labor, but they made enough money to have a pretty good life. They lived frugally, always remembering the poverty that they fled from. A two-bedroom bedroom apartment was affordable by splitting the rent.

Over time Jay understood Johnny's aversion to homosexuals, so he had never made overtures to Johnny and he was careful not to bring his lifestyle home to their apartment.

Johnny noticed that Jay was very good with money. He always seemed to have more money than he could have earned in the fields or orange groves. He wondered where Jay came up with the extra cash, but was never curious enough to ask about it. Johnny always came home tired and found that his relaxation came at the bottom of a glass of whisky. Jay worried that Johnny was falling into his father's pattern of alcoholism, so Jay would head off by himself in the evening. Again, Johnny noticed this tendency, but was comfortable with his whisky. The only thing that bothered him about Jay was his affinity for drugs. Often he would come home high on something. Ironically, in Johnny's twisted mind drugs were evil, but alcohol was acceptable.

One evening, Johnny decided to stop and have a drink after work. He was headed into a local bar when he spotted Jay walking into a bar directly across the street. He sat near the window, curious to see how long Jay would be in the bar. He sat sipping his whisky for several hours and Jay had still not come out. Curiosity overcame him, so he crossed the street and slipped quietly into the bar to see if he could spot Jay. Dim lights and a smoky atmosphere prevented him from seeing much at first. He took a stool by himself at the far end of the bar and ordered a drink. Once his eyes adjusted, he could see Jay behind him in the mirror. What he saw disgusted him. He and another man were slow dancing to the music on the jukebox. They were locked in an intimate embrace and Jay had a lip lock on the man. As Johnny watched, he saw Jay slipping his hand into the man's pants. Johnny wanted to vomit! At that moment he felt a hand move up his leg and male voice whispered "Hi here" into Johnny's ear. He grabbed the man's wrist and held on with a bone crushing grip. He looked the man in the eye and let him know that he would like to gut him on that very spot. Then he threw the man onto the floor, stepped over him and left the bar. Once he was out on the street, the nausea grew worse. Johnny lost the contents of his stomach, right on the sidewalk in front of that bar. He felt that tonight his world was out of his control. At the age of 24, he had never been out with a woman nor did he have the inclination to do so. But this did not mean he was queer! It sickened him to think that he was living with a man that could do such things to other men. As he walked home, his anger intensified. He hated queers. He hated queers! And he was living with one right under his own roof.

Johnny knew that *his* behavior was not considered normal, but in his own mind, these personality abnormalities were not his fault. He was born with them. Whatever was going on in his head connected sex to death.   It was an uncontrollable urge that would later lead to horror.

Jay's actions on the dance floor had his total attention and he had not noticed the incident. Those at the bar who witnessed it, talked about it in

Appalachian Trail After Dark
Larry Greer

great detail. So although Jay heard about the incident, he did not realize it was Johnny.

Several months later, newspapers were obsessed with stories of yet another murder in the orange groves. The stories captured everyone's attention. The murders had all been migrant workers and to make the stories more gruesome, each victim had been beheaded. None of heads were ever found. It had never been revealed in the newspaper articles, but autopsies had revealed all four victims had been sodomized. This would be the fourth unsolved murder in the Lakeland County in the past year. Migrant workers became fearful and moved on to other parts of Florida. This caused even more of an uproar, as farmers could not get their crops to market.

One night after work, rather than heading straight to his favorite bar, Jay decided to stop at home for a quick shower and change of clothes. In recent years, it had become his habit to stay out until the wee hours of the morning, preferring to spend his leisure time with men of his same persuasion. Johnny and Jay had developed very different lifestyles, so at this point the friendship had waned and they merely shared a space to live. It never occurred to Jay to wonder about Johnny's social habits. Normal or not, for this time of day, he had the apartment to himself. He could not find the shirt he wanted to wear, and thought by some chance, it might have wound up in Johnny's closet. As usual, Johnny's bedroom door was closed. When Jay opened the closet door, an unpleasant odor emanated from the bottom of the closet. Jay suspected a rat might have died in the closet and wondered how Johnny could stand the smell. He looked around for the rodent, moving clothes out of the way and spotted two five gallon containers at the back of the closet. The odor intensified and he decided this must be its source. He lifted the lid on one of the containers. It was filled with murky fluid and he realized that he had been right. The odor was making him nauseous, but curiosity made him explore further. He turned the bedroom light on to get a better look. Just under the surface of the liquid he could see something in the bucket. Cautiously he reached in with two fingers and took hold of what turned out to be hair. He pulled on the object. It rolled in the liquid and a fermented dark-skinned face emerged to stare back at him. Jay bolted backwards, realizing he had just touched a severed head.

Chapter 15
Saturday Morning February 17th

Hawk and Sam had not sleep at all during their second night at the Blood Mountain Shelter. They had not found Quenlyn on the trail and they were beside themselves with worry. She had disappeared without a sleeping bag and the temperature had dropped below 24 degrees during the night. They decided they would head out at first light to search for her. They would leave their packs in the shelter so they could cover more ground. Sam got out his maps and saw several side trails leading to this shelter. They were Freeman Trail Loop and the Slaughter Creek Trail. The two would split up and end up back on top by noon.

Just as they stepped out the shelter, a Union County sheriff's deputy and a ranger from Vogel Falls State Park came walking around the big boulders.

"Good morning," the deputy greeted. "Are you the two hikers that are missing your female partner?"

"Yes sir," responded Sam hopefully. "We were just about to split up and search side trails for her. Do you have any news?"

"No, unfortunately we have no news. But it is good that you are going to search for her. Before you go, could you show me the bone in this shelter that you found two nights ago?" Sam and Hawk were disappointed that the deputy and the ranger were not up here with good news about Quenlyn, but agreed to point out the bone.

Hawk dug around in the ashes with his hiking pole and found the bone just where he had left it. As he did last time, he picked it up with his kerchief and handed it to the Deputy who let it drop into a clear evidence bag. Then he turned the bag over, examining the bone from all sides. He agreed that it did not appear to belong to any kind of animal he had ever seen.

Sam and Hawk were anxious not to be delayed any longer. But the ranger put up a finger stopping them as he made a call on his radio.

"Johnson, this is Deputy Hall up here at Blood Mountain Shelter."

Ranger Johnson responded hopefully. "Is the young woman hiker up there?"

"No sir, she is not but her two cousins are headed out the side trails to search for her right now."

"We are still down here at the Woods Hole Shelter. JC and I spent the night up here. Now we have two missing persons in the general area so I have called in Sheriff Dill and he's going to organize search party. They'll be gathered by about eleven this morning down at the Slaughter Creek Trail Head. I told him that we think we have a homicide up here at the Woods Hole Shelter so a forensics team is on the way up here as well. I suggest the two fellows with you, come back down here and join the search group. I hate to be an alarmist, but if this is a homicide at Woods Hole, then that young woman could be in real danger. Even if she isn't part of whatever mayhem is going on up here, it was below freezing last night and she needs to be found.

Sheriff Joe Dill took pride in his work. The folks in Union respected him. It was easy to look up to this man, as he stood six foot four in his stocking feet. This morning he had put together a search team of twenty-eight volunteers. However, he would rely on Ranger Johnson to coordinate the group.

Johnson and his deputy Cargill knew the trails around Blood Mountain like the back of their hand and could place search party members in just the right places. Nevertheless, he wanted to be on the scene personally. Just as he was about to leave his office he got a call from an Atlanta Journal Newspaper reporter.

"Sheriff, this is Bill Abrams from the Atlanta Journal. Sir, I heard that you may have another murder up on the AT in your county. What can you tell me?"

This nosy reporter irritated Dill. "Buddy, I'm pretty busy right now and I have no body, so you can't have a murder without a body. Go chase another story." Before he could hang up, the reporter butted in again.

"Can you say anything about what is suspected to have happen up there?"

Now Dill was really irritated at this persistent newsman. "Listen buddy, I'm not sure where you are getting your information, but I'm not in the habit of commenting on rumors."

"Well Sheriff, I have been in touch with Robert Chandler's family and they are telling me that he is missing from a hike at Blood Mountain and that the rangers have not been able to report anything about his whereabouts. Could this be the homicide you are working on?"

"I'll tell you one more time, I don't have time for your nosy inquiries. You are only hindering any progress we might be making. Now goodbye!"

"So Sheriff, are you telling me that..." And that was the last word Dill heard as he slammed down his phone.

Given the information shared by Sheriff Dill, Sam and Hawk instead decided to hike back down the mountain towards the Woods Hole shelter. The Sheriff's comments added to their worry about Quenlyn's safety. They knew they needed to get in touch with Quenlyn's family, but did not have access to a phone. They were hopping that someone would be willing to take one of them down to the nearest pay phone. Quenlyn's father had not been in favor of his daughter going on this trip in the first place. He would not be happy with Sam, but he needed to know what had happened before he heard something on the news.

As they walked back down the trail towards the Woods Hole Shelter, Hawk and Sam stopped at a large flat rock beside the trail that offered a view of the Suches Valley. While basking in the sunshine for a moment to warm their weary bones, Hawk looked down. There was a ledge that would be a good waiting spot. He spied an energy bar wrapper...exactly the brand they had brought with them. Quickly he scrambled down to the ledge and held up the wrapper to get Sam's attention. "Sam, this is the same brand of bar we brought on the hike. Is it possible that Quenlyn was sitting here yesterday while she was waiting for you to come down the trail?"

Sam agreed that this was a good sign.

"Hey," Hawk blurted out, "look here. Do you see what I think I'm seeing?"

"I don't see anything."

"Look at those leaves. It looks to me like there has been a disturbance like maybe something, or someone has been dragged over this ground and back out onto the trail."

"Wow, you have a keen sense of observation, Hawk. Now that I look at it closer, I agree. We need to get the ranger back up here to take a look. It could be important."

When they arrived at the intersection of the Slaughter Creek side trail and the AT, they were told by a ranger to wait until the search party arrived. This frustrated Sam and Hawk. They wanted someone to share their sense of urgency in finding their beloved cousin.

Chapter 16
The Florida Cruelty

Johnny had begun to drink more heavily. He was now no longer picking fruit in the groves, but had taken advantage of working in the packing houses and it was there that he began to drink during the day. He did his work quietly and didn't mingle with other workers, who were mostly immigrants. Aspiring to become a supervisor held no interest for him. He just wanted to make enough money to buy his booze and pay his half of the rent. He had managed to save enough to buy a twelve year old Ford truck and that was the only thing he actually owned.

Even though he and Jay had shared an apartment for almost ten years, since his visit to the gay bar, Johnny had become more and more withdrawn and communicated very little with Jay, who had his own social life. Although he kept it to himself, Johnny's loathing of Jay's lifestyle increased. Jay had left the orange groves as well and had taken a job as a bartender. This job fit his lifestyle and allowed for the late night hours he liked to keep. Since he slept late into the afternoon and was gone by the time Johnny got home from work, they almost never saw each other.

Today, Johnny decided that rather than sit in the apartment and drink, he would head to a bar he sometimes frequented. He would shower off the grime from the packing shed and head out. He found the front door unlocked. Unfortunately this meant that Jay was home. He opened the door and heard retching from the bathroom. Jay was hovered over the commode throwing up. As he walked toward the bathroom to see what was wrong with Jay, he noticed that his closet doors were open.

"Something make you sick?" he sneered at Jay

Jay, not realizing that Johnny had seen the open closet doors, turned and glared at him, with a look of horror on his face.

"You – your a monster!!"

"What?" Johnny asked innocently. "What are you taking about?"

Jay was still leaning over the commode with slobber coming from the corner of his mouth.

"You know very well what I'm talking about. Those- those heads you have in your room. I can't believe I'm living with you. Where did you get them and why the Hell do you keep them in your closet?"

"Oh, calm down Jay. Your imagination is probably jist runnin' wild," Johnny cooed.

"Calm down? What do you mean my imagination is runnin' wild. I'm callin' the police."

As a child, Johnny's experience with both his father and the police, had created an irrational fear of authority figures. He could tell from Jay's expression that he would do just as threatened. Johnny could not allow that to happen.

Without saying another word, Johnny moved away from the bathroom door and stepped into his bedroom. He opened a chest draw and pulled out a knife with a 10-inch blade. He then calmly walked back towards the bathroom where Jay was now washing his face with cold water. Without a word, Johnny took the knife from behind his back and grabbed Jay's long hair. With one motion, Johnny yanked Jay's head back and sliced through his neck, nearly severing Jay's head completely. Before Jay's body even hit the floor, Johnny had pushed it into the tub. He turned on the water so that the blood from his neck could drain easily.

Then with a practiced air, Johnny walked to the front door and snapped the lock. He did not panic and did not break into a sweat. He efficiently pulled four black trash bags from the broom closet and headed into the bathroom.

He took Jay's severed head and placed it face up in the sink for draining. Seeing Jay's eyes staring at him, still with look of horror on his face gave, Johnny a feeling of complete satisfaction. He could hardly wait for the next steps in his ritual.

Chapter 17
Robert Chandler

Bob's ambition from time he was a young boy had always been to hike the entire Appalachian Trail. He was already planning a through-hike the spring after he graduated from college. Having spent time at Tec on the track team, he was in good shape. His forays into the mountains on weekends helped build his endurance.

Saturday February 10th. Bob he had planned to do a 31.7 mile speed hike from Springer Mountain north, to Neel's Gap. He knew he could do it in one day, but he wanted to try out some of his new trail gear so he would divide it into two days. His friend had dropped him off at Amicalola Falls where a blue trail led to the top of Springer Mountain. After spending Saturday night by himself on Springer, he would hit the first leg of the trail north early Sunday morning. It was a cold February day but he had worn shorts, knowing that by walking fast his body would heat up. He was carrying 18 pounds that consisted mostly of his sleeping bag, a rain suit, a clothes and ready to eat food. He would not carry a stove. Unfortunately, he would discover too late, that he had forgotten to pack a couple of essentials.

Bob had decided to wear his light track shoes, which were good for making speed. This may not have been such a great idea since the trail was rocky in many places and he ran into snow on the second day. This meant he would feel every step since his light hiking shoes did not afford him the protection that boots would have.

Gooch's Gap was 15.8 miles north and his two o'clock arrival on Sunday meant that he had made very good time. Even though he had plenty of daylight left, he decided to stop at the shelter and rest. He had brought along a book that he had torn in half feeling that would be enough to read without the extra weight.

Monday morning February 12th he knew that it would be a long gradual hike up to the top of Blood Mountain, at 4,400 feet...the highest peak in Georgia. This would be a 1,300 foot gain in elevation. The descent from Blood Mountain to Neel's Gap, was 2.4 miles. He would expect his friend Joe Wheeler to pick him up there at the mountain store around three o'clock. So far he had not met any hikers headed south.

Monday started out as a beautiful morning. The sun was out and the temperature was in the forties by noon. Unfortunately, Bob realized that even in good weather on this rocky trail, the thin-soled track shoes had not been the best idea. His feet were taking a beating on the stony path and if by chance he hit a trail snake, in these thin shoes, he could experience an injury.

He was making good time again today and would soon be passing the short side trial leading out to the Woods Hole Shelter. What he had not realized was that a lot of snow had piled up at the higher elevations. It was around one thirty in the afternoon when the unforeseen happened. Bob stepped on a lose rock under the snow and twisted his ankle. He heard it snap and knew this could be a serious injury, so he limped over to a fallen log and sat down to take his shoe off. Almost immediately, he could see the ankle swelling and his skin turning black. He knew now that he had been foolish. He could have prevented this injury if he had worn legitimate hiking boots to protect his ankles. He had been told numerous times that duct tape was a lifesaver in emergencies. Had he remembered to bring duct tape, he could have wrapped it around his ankle to reduce the swelling. A walking pole, he knew was also a good stabilizer on trails like this. In this case Bob had not thought to bring a walking stick either. Now that became an item that he must somehow find before being able to move forward.

When he put his sock back on, it was almost more than he could do to slip into his shoe, even without the shoestrings. It was excruciating and he cursed himself for being so stupid. Then the reality of his situation began to set in. He knew he was not far from the Woods Hole Shelter, but could he get himself there? If he was lucky, there would be another hiker staying there tonight. This time a year, that was an empty hope. Few hikers braved the elements on the AT in February 1973.

He spotted a fallen log about a hundred feet off the trail. The tree still had limbs attached. This was his best chance at securing a walking stick. With the aid of his new walking stick, he limped back over to his backpack and put it on. In agony, he made his way up the trail toward the shelter. Two hours later he negotiated the short distance to the shelter. What he would do after that he wasn't sure. Out of boredom he wrote in the margins of his half book:

"Monday afternoon 4:30 February 12th. Made terrible mistake, did not wear good winter boots. Took me two and a half hours to get to shelter after maybe breaking my ankle. Set up in shelter with my sleeping bag. Ankle throbbing and can no longer put weight on it. Getting dark and failed to bring light. Stupid! Can no longer see to write in the dark."

All was quiet as he tried to ignore the throbbing of his foot and get some sleep. It was then that he heard a noise outside. Then something or someone stepped up onto the shelter floor next to him.

A day later, Bob would be reported missing by his friend Joe Wheeler.

Chapter 18
The Hunt begins – Saturday, February 17th

There were now over thirty people in the Woods Hole Shelter area. In this part of the country when a call came for volunteers to help on a search party, everyone who knew the woods well responded. Maps were being distributed and searchers were told to look for any sign of a hiker that might have left the trail to look for water. Quenlyn Maguire had still not surfaced, so the volunteers were instructed to be on the lookout for both Robert Chandler and Quenlyn Maguire.

Two forensic technicians had also arrived from Atlanta and were busy assessing the situation at the shelter. They spent about two hours getting samples of the blood on the shelter floor, taking photos of the splatter pattern and carefully looking for hair or any other evidence that indicated a struggle. They found Bob's half-book inside the sleeping bag. After reading his notes written in the margins, they took finger prints from the pages and handed the book to Sherriff Dill.

When Ranger Johnson turned the search parties lose with their walkie-talkies and instructions, Sherriff Dill called to the two rangers, and motioned for Hawk and Sam to join them.

"At this point, we don't know if there is a connection between these two missing hikers, but I think we have to see that as a possibility. It appears the Chandler boy went missing several days ago and the Maguire woman disappeared yesterday afternoon. We won't know until forensics gives us the results of their findings, but my belief is that the Chandler boy was here in this shelter. Again, we have no proof, but this appears to be a crime scene and whoever was in that sleeping bag may well be dead. The forensic guy told me that the blood was probably three to four days old and because of the splatter pattern, it was most likely a blow to the head. Head wounds bleed profusely, even if they are not fatal.

"Our next step is to call out the bloodhounds. We can give them a scent of both individuals and that is a very positive step in our search."

Sam and Hawk hung around the Sheriff after the meeting was over, to ask him a question.

"Sheriff," Sam said, "We really need to let Quenlyn's parents know about what has taken place.

I know they will want to come up to the area to be here when Quenlyn is found."

"I agree" Sheriff Dill told them. "I'll handle that myself. I'll need their names and phone number." I also need to advise the Chandler boy's parents before they hear something in the paper. There's a reporter from the Atlanta Journal snooping around this story."

Chapter 19
Quenlyn Maguire

It was Friday afternoon February 16th. Quenlyn had grown tired of sitting around waiting for Sam to come back from Neel's Gap. He had left that morning to alert the rangers about what they had found at the Woods Hole Shelter. Since it had stopped snowing and the sun was out, she decided she'd go meet Sam.

"Hawk, I think I will walk a ways up the trail and wait for Sam to come back down. He must be on the way by now. I'll find a sunny spot on the trail and just enjoy the view."

Hawk who was busy breaking twigs for his fire, absentmindedly replied, "Sure, go ahead." Jokingly he added, "It won't be too many hours before dark, so don't make me have to come looking for you."

With that, Quenlyn put her jacket on, stuffed two energy bars in her pockets and attached a quart bottle of water to her utility belt. That was the last Hawk saw of her.

It was so quiet Quenlyn could hear herself breathing as she leisurely made her way back up the

Blood Mountain trail. Things were not going as planned. They should have been well on their way to Springer Mountain today, but here they were caught up in the search for a missing hiker. The thought occurred to her, that darkness would soon be upon them and they would not be able to stay at Woods Hole Shelter. They had not brought along tents and were dependent on the shelters. Luckily, the two shelters were only a mile and a half apart. That would probably mean that they'd have to hike back to the Blood Mountain Shelter tonight. She hated the thought of having to hike back up that mountain after dark. This delay would put them at least one day behind their schedule.

About one mile up the trail, Quenlyn spotted a big flat rock just off the south side of the trail. The sun was low in the western sky, but still shinning on the rock, creating a nice place to catch the sun's rays and wait on Sam. She sat down close to the rocks edge which was not but a few feet off the ground, so she hung her legs over the edge and broke into one of the energy bars she had brought along. That would take care of her hunger pangs. After the bar was gone she scooted up on the rock and lay down. She was not totally comfortable so he took the hood off her coat and rolled it up for a small pillow.

Quenlyn felt like taking a nap, but she did not dare to go to sleep and risk missing Sam coming down the trail. With her knees bent to her chest, she dropped her head to her knees and closed her eyes listening to the sounds of the forest. A woodpecker was busy hammering on the trunk of a dead tree. Crows were arguing in a pine grove nearby and a dog could be heard barking somewhere down in the valley. Occasionally a light wind whistled through the tree tops. It was about as peaceful a scene as you could find. She had been there over an hour and at four-thirty the temperature had dropped into the mid forty's. It would drop at least another ten degrees when the sun went completely down.

Quenlyn was not asleep, but she was not awake either. Pleasant thoughts were skipping through her brain when she heard a different sound...a sound of heavy breathing that was not her own. Her adrenalin triggered chills up her back. She was afraid to open her eyes, wondering if a bear was standing near her. She felt frozen to the rock itself. Now the heavy breathing was even closer. She could feel it on her face and in her ears. This was not a bear, but she still knew she was in imminent danger and she also knew she was defenseless. She opened her eyes just slightly and what she saw was the blade of a very large shiny knife. The blade was about ten inches long and glinted in the sunlight. The tip of the knife was only about six inches above her face. Her eyes followed the blade to a very dirty hand with filthy fingernails griping the handle. To see the face that the hand belonged to she would have to lean her head backwards. This was a risk she was not ready to take. Whoever was kneeling behind her could see her peering at the knife in the blade's reflection. A deep crusty voice whispered in her ear.

"Don't yo make a sound or I'll cut yo pretty little head off its shoulders. Yo understand? If yo do, blink yo eyes." Quenlyn could not have moved even if she had wanted. She blinked twice.

"I gonna to lay my knife down for a minute, so yo be very still and if you let out a scream, yo is dead, and that's fo' sure." Again he wanted to make sure she understood. Quenlyn shook her head slightly indicating she understood.

There was a ripping sound behind her which she soon realized was duct tape. He placed one piece over her mouth and the other he put over her eyes. She had not yet caught a glimpse of her captor.

Chapter 20
The Apartment

Jay and Johnny's apartment in Lakeland Florida was on the first floor of a three story building on Oak Street. There was a narrow ally that ran besides the building leading to space in the back for limited parking. It was there that Johnny kept his pickup truck. The wooden building was in bad need of paint and general repair. A single front door opened into a hallway and stairs that lead up to the other two floors. The first door to the left led into Johnny and Jay's apartment. The neighborhood housed a mixture of races that left each other alone. No one was bothered by the beer cans or trash left on the sidewalk from the night before. On hot nights, most windows were left open in the hopes of catching a breeze. Residents would sit on the steps talking while children played under the street lights. In the 1940's, the only place air conditioners could be found was in ritzy department stores.

Occasionally loud voices could be heard through the paper-thin apartment walls, but people minded their own business. Most were tolerant of the weekend music as long as it stopped by two am.

It was in this setting that Johnny felt he could perpetrate his evil deeds and go unnoticed.

Johnny 's eyes dilated as he took a hair brush from the bathroom medicine cabinet and tried to lay Jay's silky blond hair back down in the way Jay had always worn it. He stood there for a moment, and looked down into Jay's milky eyeballs.

"Jay, I'm sorry 'bout this. But I jist couldn't let you call the police. After all, I never tol' 'bout the awful things you did in that bar. You just shouldn't ha' said you'd go to the cops!"

By now all the blood had drained out of Jay's head, leaving his complexion a ghostly white. Having apologized to Jay, Johnny continued his deadly ritual. He turned his attention to the rest of Jay's body, which was now also entirely devoid of blood. Johnny's next step was to strip the body of it clothes. The big knife came in handy. Then he pulled the body partially out of the tub with the legs hanging over the edge. It was then that he performed his act of necrophilia.

Johnny was always exhausted after this step, so he left the corpse in the tub. He gently took Jay's head and put it on top of the chest that stood against the wall at the end of his bed. From his bed he could look into the dead man's eyes and imagine they were staring back at him. It was with this thought, he fell asleep.

The next morning was Friday so he dressed as usual and went to work. Jay's corpse would have to stay where it was until Saturday morning. When Johnny got up Saturday morning he made some toast and coffee. As he sat there, he realized that the smell was beginning to fill the rooms, and he feared that the next door neighbor might report this to his landlord. Jay's body had to be disposed of!

The heavy-duty black plastic bags he had removed from the broom closet on Thursday evening were still sitting in the bathroom. He stuffed one inside the other for extra strength. Once again, he checked the door to make sure it was locked. Perhaps he waited too long. Dozens of big black flies had gotten into the apartment and were now buzzing loudly in the bathroom. Johnny swatted at them to no avail, so gave up and focused on the disposal of Jay's corpse. Being in close proximity to the body he realized, just how horrific the stench had become. Other than worrying about his neighbor's reaction, the odor did not faze Johnny. With all the blood drained, he was now able to begin taking the corpse apart limb by limb. He took pleasure in cutting the flesh off the bones and putting into the bags. He had never actually seen the inside of a human body and he studied it with fascination as he continued his grizzly task.

When finished, he had four manageable trash bags that he could carry out to his truck one at a time. In an urgency to get the body out of his apartment, he risked moving the garbage bags in broad daylight. As it happened, no one noticed. He spotted some trash bags that were piled in the parking area and piled them on top of Jay's body parts. The city dump was about ten miles out of Lakeland. He climbed in the pick-up, not having bothered to change his close after his butchery. When he entered the dump he was directed to the location in the landfill used for trash and lawn debris, without garnering any suspicion. He dumped the bags that held Jay's corpse down into the pit and when he was less than 300 yards away, a bulldozer covered the bags with dirt.

Johnny then went back to his apartment and placed Jay's severed head into one of the two five gallon cans. He now had five heads in his collection. Still in the clothes stained with blood and body fluids, Johnny poured himself a drink. He was thinking about what it was going to be like to live without Jay.

Chapter 21
Return to Georgia

In 1963, Johnny was 48 years old. He'd had enough of Florida. Although he never worried that his evil deeds would catch up with him, he had a sense that it was time to move away. After Jay was no longer with him, he left the citrus packing house and had taken a job with a lumber company driving trucks. He now had experience that would help him get another job trucking somewhere in Georgia. Since he had run away at the age of 13, he had not had contact with his mother or his sister. He had no clue even if they were alive. He thought his sister might be living but he did not have any idea how to go about looking for her.

After making his mind up to quit his lumber job, he loaded his meager belongings, including the five gallon buckets, into his old truck and headed north for LaGrange, Georgia. Centerville, where he had last lived as a boy, was about five miles west of the city. He wanted to see the old home place. He did not want to confront his Pa after all these years, but he did feel a strong need to see his Ma, who had always loved him.

Two days after leaving Florida, he drove his old pick-up truck down the little country road that led out to the only home he had ever known At first he was confused. Where the house had once stood, there were now only tall weeds and the eight foundation rocks that the house had once sat on. He got out of the truck and walked over to the foundation stones and it became apparent that the house had burned to the ground years before.

Johnny knew that Elsey had probably married and moved away, but where? He wondered how to go about locating her. He obviously could not go down the road and ask Jay's parents. They would only want to know about where their son was. Then the thought occurred to him that maybe somebody at the country store might have some information.

Even the country store was different after thirty-five years. It had been remodeled and now they even sold gas. He entered the store cautiously, but did not recognize anyone. He walked around the store and back to the meat department. There he saw and old man cutting meat that look vaguely familiar. He did not want to give his name, but spoke to the old man.

"How yo doing?" He said softly, displaying an uncharacteristic smile.

"I'm just fine, can I help you?"

"Yo maybe can. Do you remember the Greene family that lived down the road? I saw where their house burned."

"Oh yes, very sad that those folks did not make it out of the house. They suspect it was the coal stove somehow caught the roof on fire. That Mrs. Greene was a regular customer and never missed spending her ten dollars. You a relative?"

"No, just knew 'em when I was young." Johnny replied quickly. The revelation of what happened to his parents shook Johnny, but he knew better than to show any emotion. He had loved his mother and sister, and had missed them greatly over the years.

"There was a girl too. I think she was their daughter. Was she in the fire too." Johnny inquired, as casually as he could.

"No, as I remember, she'd just gotten married."

"I'm sorry to keep botherin' yo, but do yo reckoned where she moved?"

"If you go into LaGrange and ask Jim Smith at the feed store on Vernon Street, he could tell you. I think he is her brother-in-law. He would know if anybody does."

It had been 35 years since Johnny had seen his sister, Elsey. She would be around 50 years old now. Why Johnny felt a need to contact her he did not know.

He walked into the feed store. A few farmers were sitting near the back smoking and chewing the fat. He walked over and asked.

"Any of yo Jim Smith?"

"No, but maybe his sister-in-law back there on the loading dock can tell you where he is."

"Thanks," Johnny replied

Johnny felt a jolt of anticipation, knowing that he was about to see his sister again after so many years. He walked out to the back where the trucks loaded their feed. He spotted a woman sweeping the dock. He had a chance to get a good look at her before she noticed him standing in the doorway. Even at 50, he recognized her.

"Elsey, that yo?"

She looked up and stared at the man that she thought looked a little familiar.

"Well yes, that's my name."

"I'm sure you couldn't recognize me, but I'm your brother."

Elsey stood there speechless, staring at the man with a scruffy gray beard, wearing bib overalls and muddy boots. The last time she had seen her brother, he had been not quite 14 years old. Now he looked like her father had when she was growing up. She thought maybe she should hug him, but Elsey was a still little reluctant.

"Johnny!!! Is that really you? I thought that you must be dead after all these years. Where have you been?

"I been in Florida."

"All this time?"

"Ya. I'm sorry I never been back. I drove out to the ol' house and saw that it had burned." Then he explained how he had found her.

"Johnny, that's been over twenty years ago. Poor Mom and Dad never made it out of the house."

Elsey asked Johnny if he would like to come to her house for supper and she would give him a bed for the night. Her husband was out of town for a few days and he was welcome.

Later that evening they were eating, Johnny told Elsey about his life in Florida. Of course he only shared the work he had done and not the life he really led. He told her he had never married. He'd worked in the orange groves and then driving trucks for a lumber company. While they were catching up, Elsey let him know that there had been some life insurance from the lumber company where their father had worked. The insurance had named both the children as beneficiaries if both parents were dead.

"Johnny, according to the will, we were to each get one half of ten thousand dollars. Your half is being held by the LaGrange Bank. Since no one knew if you were alive or how to find you, they were to hold the money for 30 years. That money is still there, waiting for you. It does have one stipulation: the bank could allocate two hundred dollars a month until the policy was all paid in full to you. All you have to do is to go the bank with me tomorrow and I will tell them who you are.

Johnny told Elsey that he was looking into a job that was available with a lumber company up near Suches, Georgia and if got it, he planned to move there. He did not want anyone to be able to find out where he lived or anything about him for obvious reasons. He knew that he did not want to cause his sister any trouble, so he decided it was better to not live near her. He asked Elsey if she minded handling the monthly check for him. She could cash it and forward the cash to general delivery at the Suches post office. She did not understand his need for privacy, but thought better about asking too many questions.

"By the way, why was it set up for such small payments?"

"Well, Pa was angry when you ran away. He always thought you would come back. I know he was not easy to live with but in his own way, I think he loved you. You'd been gone for about ten years when he stipulated how the money was to be distributed. I think that was his way of punishing you for not coming home."

Johnny just grunted. The idea that his old man had actually cared about him was too much for him to comprehend.

Two days later he drove up to Suches. It was really just a cross roads community located in a high mountain valley. When you had seen the Wolf Pen Hardware Store, the US Post Office and a small grocery, you had seen all of Suches. On occasion, there were motorcycle clubs that delighted in the curvy Wolf Pen stretch of highway. They would stop in Suches and camp out in the local fields for the weekend. That was as exciting as it got. Because the area was so remote, Georgia Highway Patrolmen didn't make it to Suches very often. The bikers loved that.

The lumber company that hired Johnny was in a very remote area of North Georgia. Driving a truck for this lumber company, he would get to know the backwoods very well and it was on one of these forays gathering lumber that he found the isolated little cabin and discovered it actually was part of the lumber company's vast tracks of forest land.

He could see that it had been abandoned for many years and figured whoever built the cabin either owned it before the lumber company bought the land or never asked permission to occupy it. So Johnny didn't ask permission either. It was located off Slaughter Creek Road, a road that had almost been forgotten by time. Because of his obsessive desire for privacy, it was the perfect place for him to carry on his abysmal way of life.

Johnny never let anyone in Suches get close to him. The most they knew about him was his name. No one knew where he came from or where he actually lived. When his lumber mill job ended he became a recluse who was occasionally seen riding a dilapidated bicycle into town. People speculated that he had had some kind of confrontation with the company in Blairsville and they ran him off.

Johnny loved to hunt small animals and an occasional deer. He had no refrigeration so he would smoke his meat. He knew the surrounding highlands and trails like no one else in the area. He would roam the mountains late at night during the warm months and sleep late in the day. He prided himself on his ability sneak up on people and animals. He would practice his art of stealth, seeing just how close he could get to backpackers on the trail and the shelters during the early hours of the morning. He would sometimes creep up to a shelter around three or four in the morning and watch the sleeping hikers. There had been a number of reports in the past few years that hikers felt someone stalking them. But, because there was no proof, it had never really been taken seriously by the rangers.

Chapter 22
The AT After Dark

Johnny Greene never stood much of a chance to lead a normal life. Between the extreme poverty of his family and his father's predilection for drink and violence, at a young age Johnny retaliated by finding pleasure causing pain and death to animals and finally to people. Today this need to kill and mutilate without remorse would be diagnosed as schizotypal or psychotic disorder. Because he also suffered from long bouts of depression, he would probably have also been diagnosed with bipolar disorder. Although Johnny felt no remorse for his killing, he knew the difference between right and wrong and this conflict drove him to alcohol dependency at an early age.

The week of February 12th 1973, was the beginning of the end for Johnny. Two young people unknown to each other hiking the AT from opposite directions would enter into Johnny Greene's world where their uncertain fate would lie in his hands.

On Monday February 12th, Bob Chandler had broken his ankle and with great pain, had struggled to make his way the short distance to the Woods Hole Shelter. Once there, he found himself in a terrible dilemma. There were almost no hikers during the cold month of February and those that came up or down the trail, might not walk off the AT to the Woods Hole Shelter. It had always been used for overflow hikers during the warmer months when the Blood Mountain Shelter was full. His first thought was to stay in the shelter overnight and get back out on the AT in the morning hoping to encounter a day hiker. He thought he might not make it long enough in the shelter if he waited for his friend to send out a search party after he didn't show up at Neel's Gap store.

But he never got the chance to put his plan into effect.

About midnight, Johnny Greene crept up to the shelter, not realizing the young man sleeping alone in the shelter was injured. That would not have made any difference to Johnny even if he had he known it. He'd been drinking for hours and had slipped into one of his killing moods. There had been no new victim now for over two years and tonight he had an uncontrollable compulsion that he could never understand. He had left his cabin and took a deer trail up the mountain to the shelter. The last two times he had visited the Woods Hole Shelter, there had not been anyone sleeping there. But tonight he'd gotten lucky. Someone was snoring lightly. From the sound of the snoring, he figured it was a young man.

Ever since the age of thirteen, he had kept the lead pipe that Jay had given. It was his memento of the old hobo's death...his first real kill. Tonight, Monday February 12th, he had it in his hand as stepped up on the shelter's platform. The muscles in his arm tensed as he moved closer to the inert form lying in the darkness. Unexpectedly, the young man in the sleeping bag rose up on one elbow. Johnny did not wait. He took a swing towards Bob's forehead and hit him just hard enough to knock him unconscious. Like clockwork, Johnny put duct tape over Chandler's blood covered eyes and mouth. Then he tied a rope around his wrists and secured them behind his back. It was not long before Chandler woke from the blow to his head. Now he hurt all over. What on earth had happened to him? In total darkness, Johnny pulled him to a standing position. This was extremely painful because of his injured ankle. He'd gone to sleep in his clothes so Johnny gave him a push to make him step off the shelter's platform floor. Chandler let out a loud cry under the duct tape as he hopped on one foot. In the moonlight, Johnny could see him pointing to his right foot. The stick that Chandler had used for a crutch was laying there on the shelter floor, so

Johnny cut his hands free and handed him the crutch. Realizing that getting Chandler to walk on the trail without being able to see, was not going to work. So he took ripped the duct tape from his eyes and ordered him to start walking. As an extra precaution, Johnny tied a rope around Bob's neck so he could not get away.

The pain in Chandler's ankle was almost more than he could bare, but this did not faze Johnny in the least. It took almost three hours to get down the mountain. It would soon be daylight when Chandler stumbled through the front door of the dark cabin. He stood leaning on his crutch watching Johnny light the lantern. There was still fire in the fire place so Chandler was directed to sit down on the only chair and face the fire while Johnny stoked it with more logs. Then Johnny ripped the tape off Chandler's mouth and handed him a glass of water. He drank the water gratefully, even thought he could see the lack of cleanliness of the glass. Chandler had to know what was going on. In a hoarse voice he asked,

"Who are you and why have you brought me here?" Silence! Johnny's face had the expression of someone trying to come up with an answer. When he did speak it almost sounded like a confession.

"Ya see --- I have dese demons in me dat makes me do things that I can't 'splain, even to myself. Don't think I'm normal."

None of this made sense to Bob. "Why would you nearly kill me and then force me to hobble all the way down that mountain with a broken foot. I'm in a lot of pain and it is getting worse."

"If I had done what I had really planned to do, yo wouldn't be talkin' now."

"What had you planned to do?" Bob wasn't quite sure he wanted to hear the answer.

"Well, since ya won't be leavin' this place, I'll tell ya. I collect heads and since it was so far up on dat mountain, I 'sided to let ya walk yo'self down here cause you's too heavy to drag that fa'."

"You collect heads? What kind of heads?"

"Is yo stupid? I means heads like is on yo shoulders, dat's the kind of heads I be talking 'bout."

This revelation shook Chandler. He realized he was indeed in the hands of a madman. When he looked around, he could see stains on the big table in the dim light. His imagination went wild. Little did he know that what he was thinking was not far from the truth? Johnny noticed Chandler squirming and could read his thoughts. That pleased his demented mind.

Johnny looked down at Chandler and grinned through his nasty beard. He took two steps over to the wall to the five lidded buckets that held his gruesome collection of heads.

He knew Bob was watching him, so he slowly opened up one of the buckets and laid the lid aside. Bob was nearly in tears fearing what he was about to see. Johnny stuck his hand into the liquid formaldehyde and grabbed the hair of the head that was nearest the top. As he slowly pulled it up, he let the fluid drain a little before turning around and letting Chandler see what he was holding. He walked toward Chandler with the dripping head. The smell of the fluid and its contents was doing a number on Chandler's stomach. He shut his eyes and gagged.

Johnny ignored Chandler's discomfort, continuing to explain who the person had been. "This here is Jay. He was my best friend until he decided to call the police. He may be dead, but I still have good memories of him when we was boys. We was neighbors and hobo'd to Florida together. He was a queer, but I kinda looked the other way."

Chandler was now paralyzed with fear. He wanted to scream, but who would ever hear him? This exhibition of Johnny's told him what fate he would face. With the injury, he had no chance to escape this Frankenstein cabin in the wilderness.

Johnny put a blanket on the floor near the fireplace and told Chandler he could lie down and sleep if he wanted to. There was a dog chain hanging on the wall which Johnny took down and secured around Chandler's broken ankle and attached the other end to one of the big table legs. Then he removed a hammer from the wall and drove large nails into the floor and bent them over portions of the chain. Now Johnny felt he could sleep without worrying Chandler might escape.

Johnny was very tired after a long night so he took his bottle of Jim Bean off the shelf and poured a half glass with a splash of water. Something human in him made him offer Chandler more water. Still in a filthy glass, but Chandler drank.

Feeling confident that Chandler was not going anywhere, Johnny lay down on his bed, but then got back up and found a small pail and put it at

Chandler's side in case he needed to pee. He then crawled back on his bed and fell fast asleep. Bob did not sleep. He was terrified of this man. He thought he had a good idea of what he planned to do, but when? The wound to his head was throbbing and his ankle was beginning to look gangrenous. In this condition he knew he could not get away. If somehow he did get out the cabin door without being detected, it would only be a matter of time before he was caught. His situation was hopeless. This is where he would die!

The abduction of Chandler had not gone as Johnny had planned. He had just wanted to hit the victim in the head just hard enough to knock him unconscious. He was unhappy that he had struck the victim's head so hard. The pipe had made an ugly gash on Chandler's forehead and a lot of blood had been left on the shelter floor. Johnny was unhappy about this because he was looking forward to another nice trophy to preserve. He would normally drain the blood from the head and keep it on a shelf for several days to admire before preserving it. But this head was not going to look good given the damage done by the lead pipe. Maybe if he kept Chandler alive for a while, the wound would heal and then he could carry out his original plan.

Snow had continued through the night and into Tuesday. Johnny's escapades had exhausted him and he slept soundly until after two pm. The fire had gone out and Chandler was curled up in a blanket that was barely keeping him warm. He had not slept at all as his right leg was throbbing. It had definitely gotten worse during the night. He was numb with thoughts about what would the day bring.

When Johnny finally woke he rebuilt the fire. After he had a good blaze, he went over to the shelf where he kept his food. He found some crusty rolls and a jar of peanut butter. He spread peanut butter onto four hard rolls. Two of them he put on a tin plate and set them on the floor in front of Chandler. Bob had watched Johnny's every move and thought the offering was probably inedible, but his fear of the man prompted him to eat the rolls. Johnny left the cabin and was gone for several hours. He did not return until after dark. Johnny checked to see if Chandler had attempted an escape, but saw no evidence. That night before settling into his nightly ritual of whisky, he opened two cans of sardines and two cans of pork and beans. He poured half of each onto the same unwashed tin plate and set it in front of Chandler with an unwashed spoon. Although this was the first food of the day, he ate without appetite.

Johnny knew these mountains like no other person in the area. He knew all the deer trails and often used the ones that paralleled the AT. He was stealthy and fit. By traveling lite, he could cover great distances in relativity little time. Three days later, Thursday the 15th, as the three cousins were headed south toward Blood Mountain, Greene had headed out and was walking north in the direction they were coming from. He decided it was safe to leave Chandler alone in the cabin for the day. Again, he went out in hopes of stalking new hikers. The hike north over Blood Mountain and maybe as far as Hogs Pen would not take him long. Even the heavy snow didn't bother him. It only took him two hours to crest Blood Mountain and walk down and across the highway to the mountain store breezeway. He knew the store would be closed for the winter, but there was a man working on the plumbing. He recognized the man from his visits to Suches. The man recognized him and waved as he walked through the breeze way. Johnny nodded in recognition, but kept moving. He didn't want to be distracted from his mission. On the north side of Neel's Gap precipitation had turned from snow to freezing rain as his journey took him up the trail.

After walking four miles on a deer trail that closely paralleled the AT, he spotted three hikers coming down the trail in his direction. They all had on blue rain suits. He lay down on the ground behind a fallen log about three hundred feet from the trail and watched as they made their way passed him. All three of the hikers had on their rain hoods so he was unable to see faces. He did however notice that the last one was a female.

Johnny enjoyed stalking hikers and spooking them. He would fall in behind them at a safe distance and occasionally reveal himself to the last hiker in a group. He would always make his appearance very brief and sometimes only show part of himself, perhaps peeking from behind a tree. Dark days when there was rain or fog, were his favorites.

Quenlyn Maguire was lagging behind her two cousins that afternoon. They were all tired and looking forward to reaching the Blood Mountain Shelter. She had dropped back to relive herself and was out of sight of the other two. When she was hefting her pack back onto her shoulders, she spotted movement in her peripheral view. She was sure she saw someone about three hundred yards back up the trail. He was watching her from behind a big tree. This was unnerving so she decided she needed to get closer to Sam and Hawk. The fog was dense and the freezing rain made it difficult to catch up with the guys. After a quarter mile, Sam and Hawk noticed she had fallen behind and stopped to let her catch up.

"I thought I would never catch you guys."

Hawk chuckled and asked, "Anything wrong?" There was a catch in Quenlyn's voice when she responded.

"I could swear that I saw someone stalking me back there."

"Are you serious? Sure you are not just seeing things in the fog?" Sam chided.

"I know you don't believe me, but I felt someone back up the trail. I could swear I saw someone leaning out from behind a tree watching me. Oh God, it really spooked me."

After resting in Neel's Gap, the three would cross the highway and make their way up Blood Mountain. It had begun to snow on this side of the gap. The rest of the day Quenlyn made sure she stayed between the two cousins.

Greene continued to follow at a safe distance. He was pleased with himself. He'd given that girl a good scare. He would wait for the three hikers to settle into the Blood Mountain Shelter before moving past and back down the mountain towards his cabin. The snow would cover his tracks and no one would know he had passed the shelter during the night.

It was 1 am when Hawk had heard screams reverberate across the mountains.

****

Chandler had lain on the floor in front of the fireplace all day. The warm fire had been reduced to smoldering embers. He was not close enough to the fireplace to add more wood, so he lay shivering under the light blanket. In a final act of desperation, Chandler realized, even with his manacle, nailed to the floor, he could reach the window on the back wall. By getting up on his knees, he could pull back the ragged curtain and see the snow-covered ground. He was desperate to call out for help. He looked around and saw nothing with which to knock out the window pane so he reared back and with all the strength left in his pain-wracked body and hit the window with his damaged forehead. He managed to break out half of the lower pane and re-open the wound in his head at the same time. The opening was large enough for him to stick his face out without getting cut. He wanted to get attention so he filled his lungs full of air and screamed into the darkness as loud as he could. He caught his breath and bellowed out another scream. This was the blood curdling sound that Hawk could hear as he stood near the edge of the rock outcrop on top of Blood Mountain.

Johnny had passed the Blood Mountain Shelter as he headed back to the cabin when he heard the scream. Thinking that something was probably amiss in his cabin, he ran the rest of the way in the moonlight, only to find Chandler curled up in his blanket on the floor. He was hungry so he fixed a pot of grits and put a can of tuna in it. He gave Chandler a bowl along with a cup of coffee. He studied the chain on Chandler's leg and was satisfied that he had not tried to escape. The curtain covered the broken window and so Johnny was none the wiser. The broken piece of glass had fallen to the ground outside so it was not noticed by Johnny and the wind was still so no breeze blew in to give away Chandler's attempt at rescue.

Johnny capped off his grits and tuna with a hefty shot of Jack Daniels. His plan was to go track the three hikers again the next day in hopes of catching one of them.

Chapter 23
Quenlyn's abduction

As Johnny was putting the duct tape over Quenlyn's eyes and mouth, she was thinking: "Where the Hell is Sam? He should be here by now. My God, what is this monster going to do to me?"

Johnny had never touched a woman with the exception of his Mom and sister. When he pulled her to her feet, he noticed how soft her arms felt. It was a sensation he had never experienced. Once he got her into his cabin she would never leave alive. What a trophy her head would make with all that beautiful blond hair.

Once he had her on her feet, he grabbed her left arm and warned her not to resist if she wanted to live. Quenlyn could only moan at this comment. She was terrified. If only Sam would show up now. He was strong and could handle this creep. The only disadvantage was that very big knife.

****

Johnny was certainly demented, but he was not dumb. He had survived all these years because of his ability to reason things through. Having just abducted Quenlyn, he realized he needed to change his plan. She could not be taken directly to his cabin because he realized that the two men she was hiking with would begin searching for her the minute they realized she was missing.

If he took her on his direct route to his cabin, her two companions could follow their tracks in the snow. Although not totally prepared, he decided to head for an old abandoned barn near Slaughter Gap. He would take Quenlyn there and spend the night. The next day he would retrace his steps and then head back to his cabin in the afternoon. His logic was that the two companions would not be still looking for her near the Woods Hole Shelter. The rock that Quenlyn had been resting on extended on the other side of the tail for a couple of hundred yards and their footsteps could not be followed across the surface of the rock. It would confuse anyone looking for tracks.

He took the tape off her eyes and directed her to follow him. The trail was almost non-existent and it ran for a mile and a half around the base of Blood Mountain. The barn would give some shelter from the weather. There were some lose boards on the floor so Johnny laid them beside each other and told her that was where they would sleep. He had searched her pockets finding only an energy bar and her bottle of water. He thought about eating the bar, but decided to pull the tape off her mouth let her have it.

It was a miserable night. Quenlyn was clad only in her jacket, with no blanket or gloves to keep her warm. She was not about to lay down, not being sure what he had planned for her, so she sat as far away from her abductor as she could get. After she finished the energy bar, Johnny had taped her hands and feet so she couldn't escape. He was cold as well, so he to build a small fire to keep them from freezing. He never left his cabin without matches for this very reason. Although Quenlyn was so tired she had trouble with coherent thought, she still knew enough to keep an eye on this man. She did not even doze off during that long night. Johnny on the other hand, snored loudly for several hours.

The next day, Johnny figured that if they got back to the AT around five or six o'clock it would be dark and no one would still be looking for her up there. He reasoned they would head back to Neel's Gap.

When he and Quenlyn arrived back at the spot where he had grabbed her on the AT, he decided to tape her eyes and mouth again. He just did not want to risk her screaming where there might be ears close enough to hear. Again, he warned her,

"I be walkin' right 'side you. So jist head out. I won't let you mash into a tree."

Quenlyn was remembering that her dad had suggested she take a pistol for protection, but Sam had scoffed at that idea and cautioned her about the extra weight in her pack. Was this mountain man going to rape her? If he had plans for that, why had he not already done it? He'd had his chance in the barn the night before.

She could tell that the downhill trail was steep. Too steep for a regular hiking trail, Johnny was using a deer trail that he knew well even though it was covered with snow. He wanted to avoid getting near the Woods Hole Shelter should someone still be there. He had noticed that there were a number of tracks in the snow and figured someone was looking for Chandler or this woman. He felt superior that he had outwitted them.

Suddenly, Johnny froze in his tracks. He did not say a word and Quenlyn sensed that something had happened. Johnny had very keen hearing and good instincts in the woods. He remained very still as he looked to his left towards the ridge that ran south in the area of the Woods Hole Shelter. Then the sound came again and he knew instantly that it was the baying of bloodhounds. This could only mean one thing. They were tracking this woman by her scent and possibly the hiker he had taken earlier that week. They would not have his scent, but with all likelihood the dogs would find one of these two hiker's scent. Greene had never encountered either the police or the rangers. He felt stupid. With all he had done over the years, of course the law would now be after him. In Florida he could always get into his truck after killing a migrant worker, leaving a cold trail. The police in Lakeland never worried too much about the death of migrants. Because he and Jay had lead such different lives, even Jay's queer friends would not know about Johnny or where the two had lived together in Lakeland. If he had ever been reported missing, no one would connect him to Jay.

For a moment, Quenlyn found the sound of baying hounds hopeful. They were looking for her! But that hopeful feeling lasted only momentarily. In a whisper, Greene warned her,

"Let's move! I mean faster!" He told Quenlyn. He could only think of one way to fool the dogs.

Chapter 24
The Bloodhounds of Blood Mountain

When the tracker made it up to Woods Hole, Sheriff Dill called him over.

"Hey Mose, how come it took you so long to get up here boy?"

"Well Sheriff you know I come from Bristol and that's a far piece up the road."

Sheriff Dill chuckled.

"You don't need to tell me were Bristol is. I just thought you'd be here before now."

"Well the snow is a lot deeper in Bristol and I got here as fast as I could. Coming up here on that side trail ain't no Sunday walk in the park." JC Cargill and a couple of others were standing around and got a kick out of the banter between the Sheriff and Mose Means. Mose reminded them of the deputy on the Andy Griffin show. Mose was a tall elderly black man and had a reputation as the best deer and wild boar tracker in the mountains of north Georgia. When he was not on call to track people, he would take his two hounds, Mo and Jo hunting for deer or wild boar.

Now all business, Mose asked about the assignment. He needed to know everything he could about the missing hikers.

"What we got here are two missing hikers. The one that was in this shelter is a male and the other one is a young woman. At this point, we are not sure if there is a connection between the two. The hiker that was in this shelter disappeared last Monday and the young woman turned up missing yesterday. She was hiking with those two." He jerked a thumb in the direction of Sam and Hawk. "The three are cousins."

"Is there gear or clothing I can let the dogs sniff?" The sheriff pointed into the shelter and Mose saw the sleeping bag. "Was he in the sleeping bag?"

"Sheriff, before I get the dogs all excited, I need to know which of the two people you want me to look for first."

Mo and Jo were registered Bloodhounds. According to Mose, they were the best trackers in four states.

"I think we look for the woman first. Her trail is a lot warmer, and I'm sure your dogs will pick up her scent." Hawk retrieved Quenlyn's sleeping bag and let the dogs take a good long sniff.

"Where she was last seen?" Mose asked

"Her two cousins think she walked about a half mile up the trail towards Blood Mountain Shelter. She was waiting for that tall guy to come back down the trail from the Neel's Gap store. One of them can take you to where they suspect she was waiting," Sheriff Dill offered.

Knowing that it would be a long cold night, the sheriff suggested, "Why don't you guys see if some wood can be rounded up and let's build a fire to keep warm. We can't all go follow Mose, but I suggest that JC and two of the others go as his backup. I just hope that young woman is able to find a spot out of the wind and snow tonight. I understand she only had on a jacket.

Sam volunteered to show Mose Means the spot where they had found the wrapper. He wanted to tag along with Mose and the dogs and promised not to get in the way.

"I suppose that would be OK, but remember that you're not carrying a weapon. Can't tell what you are going to run into in these woods."

Having taken a good sniff of Quenlyn's sleeping bag, Mo and Jo knew that they were being called into action. The tracking would begin at the shelter and would proceed up the AT towards Blood Mountain. When Mose spoke the words, "Let's Go", they were ready and the baying started. The dogs were excited and Moses always had to hold them back when they had a scent to follow.

Chapter 25
The Chase

Johnny was unnerved by the sound of the hounds baying near Woods Hole. He sensed that they were headed up the AT towards Blood Mountain. He was smart enough to know that they would follow the woman's scent to where he had abducted her.

He knew the woods well even after dark. But he had a woman who was blind folded and gaged. Speed was going to be his only chance to get away. He could give in and release the woman, but she had seen his face and could describe him.

Finally, he rationalized that he needed to take the tape off her eyes so they could move faster. Why he was so intent on taking her along, she didn't know? He was taking almost two steps to her one as he rushed her down the mountain. Quenlyn was clearly unable to keep up with him, but he had such a tight a grip on her arm that it was the only reason she didn't fall.

He hoped the snow would cover their tracks, but he knew that these dogs could follow a scent even through snow.

The baying back up the mountain was getting closer. Had they now found the spot where he had grabbed the woman?

Johnny wanted to head to the cabin where he felt secure, but he knew his route needed to be indirect or he'd lead the dogs straight to his hideout. His plan was to make it to the confluence of Slaughter Creek and another smaller creek near Slaughter Gap. There the creek would double in size as it flowed between Slaughter Mountain and Blood Mountain. There had been a lot of precipitation recently which increased the volume of water. His plan was to jump into the creek, follow it up stream for a ways, then turn around and come back down the creek near his cabin. His hope rested on the dogs not being able to follow the scent in the water. That was the only thing he knew to do. As they neared the confluence of the two creeks, Quenlyn could hear the water before the stream came into sight. It was not until that moment that she understood his intentions.

He stepped into the stream with his heavy, waterproof boots and pulled Quenlyn in after him. Her boots filled with water on the first step into the icy stream. She could sense just how desperate this man was to escape the hounds. Maybe he did not intend to kill her after all. Soon they were up to their knees in the black water. Footing was almost impossible and Quenlyn found it extremely difficult not to stumble and plunge into the water. Despite the cold temperatures, perspiration was forming under her clothes from the exertion.

****

Mose and the dogs were now at the spot where Sam thought Quenlyn had been sitting that afternoon. Mo and Jo were again given a piece of her clothing to smell and that was all it took. True to their reputation, the hounds chose the most recent scent and not the one coming from the direction of the barn where she has spent the previous night. *The chase was on.* Mo and Jo became almost uncontrollable as they caught the fresh scent. Their loud baying and howling echoed across the mountain. Mose was struggling to hold them back as he headed downhill in the dark. Mose was not a young man anymore and he trusted his dogs, but feared falling himself.

Johnny and Quenlyn's foot prints were being covered with snow, but this didn't stop Mo and Jo. They could smell Quenlyn's scent and knew they were close. They could smell Johnny's scent as well, but paid no attention to it. They were not after him.

145

Sam who was coming along behind, could not guess why Quenlyn would walk off the AT down into these woods that did not appear to have a trail. There was underbrush and dead falls were everywhere. Was she trying to escape something or somebody? Nobody had an answer for that, but the hounds knew they were on her scent.

The snow continued to pile up on the trail. Both the dogs and the trackers were finding it difficult to make any speed. Adrenaline was flowing through the veins of both dogs and men. The chase was both exciting and freighting because no one knew how close they were to finding the woman. Would she still be alive? Time was of the essence.

****

Johnny and Quenlyn continued to slosh through the water and make their way up a stream that was both inky black and obstructed by the snow covered branches of Mountain Laurel leaning out over the water. Quenlyn's feet were numb and she was finding it difficult to breath because of the tape over her mouth. With all the exertion, she needed to take in a deep breath but could not. After a strenuous three or four hundred yards, Johnny turned around and headed back down the creek the way they had come. Johnny had one more diversion in mind once they neared the cabin.

****

Back up on the mountainside where the trackers were moving down the slope, Mose Means was struggling hard to keep his footing and restrain the two bloodhounds from pulling away. Even without the cover of snow this hillside was hazardous. Holes left by rotted out tree stumps were covered over by leaves and snow. As experienced as Mose was, he fell prey to one of these traps. He stepped into a deep hole and heard his shin bone crack. He cried out in pain realizing he had fractured his leg. What happened next was unavoidable. In his fall, Mose lost his grip on the dogs' tethers.

The result could have been predicted. Both Mo and Jo, feeling the release, took off down the mountainside into the darkness. The dogs had been trained only to respond to Mose's voice and in his agony, he failed to call out the command to stop. JC Cargill, was right behind Mose, and stopped to help extract him from the stump hole.

"Oh God! I can't believe what just happened. JC, some of you have to go after my dogs. Two things can happen: one is that if they catch up with the woman, her abductor could kill my dogs; the other possibility is that they get confused and lose the scent. I'm not sure you can catch them now, but I hope a couple of you will go after them."

****

Cargill got on his radio and called Sheriff Dill who was waiting up at Woods Hole.

"Sheriff, Mose stepped into a stump hole and it looks like he has broken his leg. We need some help to take him down the mountain and get him to a hospital."

"We'll be right on it." Dill responded.

Back down the mountain where Mose was leaning against a tree, JC asked Sam if he would join him going after the dogs. Harry Smith a local volunteer would stay with Mose until help arrived. JC and Sam headed after the dog tracks at a steady but cautious pace. Neither one wanted to end up like Mose.

Sam had brought along both of his hiking poles so he offered one to JC. This made it easier to check the ground in front of them.

Every few minutes they could hear the howling of one or both of the dogs. JC was not trained in how to interpret the baying, but suspected they were reporting back to Mose that they were still on the scent.

****

In places the creek was almost waist deep. Quenlyn wondered how long she could continue this forced march. When she began to fall behind, Johnny turned around and became angry. He waved his knife at her.

"Move Dammit, Move!" He hollered at her.

The hound's baying had now become sporadic and their barking seemed to be less excited. Johnny was hopeful that his ruse was working. The dogs were still about a mile up the mountain, but they could close in fast. Johnny still felt the urgency to move back down the creek as quickly as possible.

****

Chandler had not seen his captor all day and now it was close to midnight. Johnny had forgotten to turn the gas lantern off before he left so Chandler had light in the cabin until a few hours before, when the wick burned out. During the day the two windows in the cabin also provided some light. The fire was now just a pile of ashes. His ankle was swollen to the knee and turning black. His earlier fear of gangrene was now certain. If by some miracle he got out of here alive, he would probably lose his leg, or just die in the hospital.

He had nothing to eat since the night before and the room was beginning to spin around him. The chain that secured to his bad ankle was nailed to the floor. If he could somehow get the nails out, he could then remove the chain from the table leg. Unfortunately, no tool was within reach that would help pry loose the nails. Chandler had given up. He curled into a fetal position and waited to lose consciousness. It was then that he heard a man's voice outside. At this point he wasn't sure if he was hallucinating or if his captor had finally returned. It sounded like he was talking to someone. Was this guy talking to himself or did he have another prisoner now?

****

"Sheriff, this is JC. Can you hear me?"

The sheriff's voice came across the radio, so JC explained the situation.

"Sheriff, the dogs are moving fast down the mountain and we haven't been able to catch them. They seem to be heading towards the Slaughter Creek Road. How about getting some backup and head down the Slaughter Creek side trail? I'll find them at the bottom. I'm not sure the two of us can handle what we might run into down there, as Sam does not have a weapon."

"I'm on it. Suggest you keep your box on mute. They tend to make a big sound that carry's at night."

JC had not had any training as a tracker in Ranger School. His training had been focused on park regulations and dealing with difficult people. Tonight he was totally out of his element. His only confidence right now, was his government issued Glock Pistol.

Chapter 26
Nearing Death

Today psychologists would tell you that only one in ten million people have the combination of psychological disorders that Johnny Greene suffered from. Unfortunately, his mental illness had escaped the notice of the people around him; and when he was a young boy mental illness was not considered treatable. The mentally ill were merely locked up. When it was important, he could function well enough to present himself in a reasonable fashion, but stress and depression would trigger his maladies leading to murder, necrophilia and cannibalism.

He could go for weeks at a time and his mind worked in an almost normal fashion. But when triggered by depression or fear, his blood pressure and heart rate would increase. He would become restless and his eyes would turn bloodshot. These symptoms were the beginning of bad spells for Johnny and death for his victims.

He knew what his intention was for the young man in his cabin; and his initial intention for the young woman was to take her to a place away from his cabin where he could remove her head and add it to his growing collection. At last count he had seven trophy heads in his five gallon buckets. Each one held special memories for him, especially his childhood friend, Jay. Tonight as he ran from the baying hounds, he was developing a severe headache affecting his ability to think and act clearly.

Like a wild beast being, Johnny was being pursued by these dogs, and was running for his life. He stumbled and nearly fell into the stream several times. Both he and Quenlyn were completely soaked and hypothermia could not be far behind.

****

Initially, JC sensed that the dogs were closing in. The terrain was so difficult that he figured whoever they were chasing must know these woods well. However, the urgency of Mo and Jo's baying had abated in the past fifteen minutes. That was puzzling. He and Sam were now walking parallel to Slaughter Creek near the point when it joined a smaller stream.

"Sam, I think the dogs are just ahead and waiting for us."

"I can hear water. Maybe they don't want cross the creek."

Sam was right. Mo and Jo were sitting patiently next to each other, waiting for further instructions.

"Sam, the dogs are looking up the creek so my guess is that Quenlyn and her captor went up stream in that direction trying to cause the dogs to lose her scent." JC had a better sense for tracking than he gave himself credit for.

"That water is petty swift," Sam observed. "And neither one of us has on the right kind of boots or clothes to be walking in water where you can't see depth. If we fell down and got totally wet, there's no way to dry off and that could prove to be fatal in these temperatures."

JC was thinking, "If they did walk up the creek for a distance to cover up their scent, they would eventually have gotten out on the other side where there is an old logging road. It is an extension of the Slaughter Creek Gap Road. If they did get on the road, they probably would head south down towards the valley. Let's take the dogs across the creek at the shallowest point and walk up the other side to see if the dogs pick up Quenlyn's scent.

Somewhere down that road, we will run into the deputies."

****

Sheriff Dill, with Hawk's help, had been able to get a message to Quenlyn's parents. It was a call no one wants to make. At first Quenlyn's father was furious with Sam and Hawk. After all Sam had talked their daughter into making this ridiculous hike in the middle of the winter. He quickly calmed down and asked directions to Suches. Quenlyn's mom and dad were headed their way. It would take them about three hours and they would arrive in the middle of the night.

The Sheriff still had very little to go on. He now knew that someone had snatched the Maquire girl, but in such a short time there were no leads about who it could be. Around midnight a ranger showed up in the staging area.

"Sheriff, I have been working to locate anyone who might have seen someone in the area of Blood Mountain. We might have gotten lucky. A plumber working down at the Neel's Gap store saw a man he knew from Suches walking through the breezeway on Thursday around noon. He figured that he must be hiking since he noticed a water bottle."

"Did you get a name from the plumber?" Sheriff Dill asked.

"Said his name is Johnny Greene and he lives somewhere in the mountains near Suches. Comes into town once or twice a month for supplies."

"Did the Plummer give you a description of this fellow?"

"Yes, said he was a kinda' creepy. Always wears dirty bib overalls and has a long grey beard. Maybe sixty years old."

The Sheriff got on his radio and called his dispatch office in Bristol. He told them that first thing in the morning, he wanted someone to check both the hardware and grocery store in Suches to see if anyone could give them more information on this Johnny Greene fellow.

Chapter 27
The Finial Diversion

JC and Sam crossed the icy stream with the two dogs and emerged on the other side. They stopped long enough to pour the water out of their boots and ring out their socks. The wind had picked up and blowing snow was making it more difficult to see in the dark. With the hounds on their tethers, they proceeded up the north bank of the creek where it appeared the trail had gone cold. Mo and Jo were still trying to do their job, but the scent had suddenly ended. JC knew that the young woman and whoever was with her had gone into the water and suspected that they had waded up the middle of the creek to avoid detection. What he wanted to do was to find where they had emerged from the creek. That would be where the dogs could again pick up the scent and continue the hunt. After walking several hundred yards, JC stopped. He told Sam that he was baffled. No one could walk this far up the creek in the freezing water and survive.

"You know, JC, just maybe they didn't come this far up the creek."

"What do you think?"

"What if they walked a short way up the creek and then backtracked down the creek, exiting below where they entered on the other side. I've read of this tactic in books when a convict was trying to evade hounds."

"You may be on to something Sam. Let's head back and go below where we started. At least we can find our trucks and warm up a little. I'm getting numb."

Around 8:15 am Sunday morning, Sheriff Dill got a call on his walkie-talkie form his dispatch office.

"Sheriff, we found two people in Suches that knew this Johnny Greene guy. They both described him as an odd duck. He comes into Suches a couple times a month for food and mail. He rides a bicycle with side bags to carry his stuff in back to wherever it is that he lives. He has been seen coming or going on the Wolf Pen Road. But that's about all those fellows know. I'm sure that if we canvased the area, someone will know more about where he lives. From what Amos at the hardware store says, Johnny probably lives in the mountains. He is very reclusive and avoids people at all costs. We did find out that up to a couple of years ago, he drove a lumber truck for the S&W lumber company up here in Bristol. We made a call to them and found out that he had left three years ago. They did still have his driver's license on file that shows a Georgia address."

"That's good work. Thanks. This morning try to find more about and get back to me."

****

Quenlyn and Johnny were now at the end of their endurance. Quenlyn was ready to give up and drop in the water, never to emerge. She no longer had any feeling in her legs and breathing only through her nostrils was freezing her lungs. She needed to breathe through her mouth, but her hands were tied behind her so she could not remove the tape.

Johnny was also near his limit. The only thing keeping him going was his adrenaline and his desperate desire to escape the dogs. If the woman he was with fell into the water, he would not bother to pull her out again. He knew she'd drown in the icy water with her mouth gagged and her hands tied behind her.

When they came around a bend in the creek, they could see three unattended sheriff's cars and two ranger trucks. It was then that Johnny formulated his final diversion to bring an end to the hunt. He directed the woman to follow him and they climbed the bank out of the creek and walked towards the vehicles. Once they were among the cars and trucks, Johnny turned around and picked up the woman carrying her back down to the creek in the same direction they had come out of the water. Once at the edge of the creek he sat her down and told her to stay quiet.

Johnny then broke off a leafy Laurel branch and headed back to the cars. He had learned to cover their tracks in the snow so as he covered his tracks, he backed back down to the creek where the woman was waiting as he had instructed. In this way her scent would only lead the dogs to the trucks and there the scent would stop. He hoped the trackers would think that the person being tracked had gotten into a car and left.

His cabin was just around the next turn and hidden view of the creek. He and Quenlyn crossed the creek for the last time. Here he picked up his near unconscious captive and headed toward his cabin.

Chapter 28
Surrounded

Mo and Jo had not picked up a scent coming back down the opposite side of Slaughter Creek. If the people on the run had exited the creek, there was no sign of it. JC was stumped, he felt exhausted and could not get back to his truck soon enough. He just wanted to sit in his truck with the heater going and take a cat nap. He had the foresight to bring a small overnight bag that contained a dry pair of socks. This small luxury sounded heavenly right now.

They were getting close to the Slaughter Creek trailhead. Cars and trucks of the rangers, officers and volunteers would be parked there. About three hundred yards down the road, the cars came into site. As they got nearer, JC and Sam could see sheriff and ranger deputies standing around either with their hands in their pockets or holding hot coffee merely for the warmth. White exhaust was coming from two of the cars indicating they too were warming up and maintaining radio contact.

When JC neared the cars with the dogs, Mo and Jo came to life. Their baying and howling startled everyone. This was the first time they had barked for some time.

"Hold on Mo," JC called out to the dog. "I do believe they have picked up the scent again right here in the parking lot. It seems to be leading up from the creek to the cars. It was there, however, that the scent ran out. The dogs sniffed in circles and came right back to where the scent was strongest. It was a dead end.

Sam feared that Quenlyn had been thrown into a car and driven away. There were a lot of car tracks in the snow with the five vehicles coming and going during the night.

Sheriff Dill, seasoned at this type of work, proposed another theory.

"Think about it for a minute. There is no way in the world that somebody was waiting here to pick them up. It just doesn't add up. If by some chance there was someone in a car about the time the man and Ms. Maguire came out of the woods, they might have forced their way into the car and taken off. But the odds of that happening up here on a morning like this, is highly unlikely."

Dill was thinking that it would take somebody who knew these woods to fool these two bloodhounds. This made him think of the mountain man Johnny Greene.

JC had turned the dogs over to another deputy while he and Sam got into his truck to warm up. One of the deputies handed them a hot thermos of coffee and a couple of sweet rolls. Nothing had ever tasted better. They were both worn out form the all-night chase and disappointed it had not resulted in finding Quenlyn. A nap would have been a wonderful thing at this time.

Hawk had been asked by the Sheriff, to stay near the shelter for the rest of the day. If someone came up or down the AT, and wanted to use the Woods Hole Shelter, he was to tell them that the shelter was closed and no one would be allowed to use it until farther notice.

****

Johnny had picked Quenlyn up at the creek side and carried her towards the cabin. He did not want the hounds to follow her scent from the creek to his doorstep. Quenlyn was nearly unconscious when Johnny reached into his bib overall pocket and removed his key. With some difficulty, he turned the key in the padlock, while keeping Quenlyn's feet from touching the snow. He pushed the door open and the stench of the musty cabin accosted her nostrils. Quenlyn could barely keep her eyes open to witness her surroundings. Regardless, she welcomed the shelter. Johnny put her down to the floor and turned to relock the door. Once the door was shut, it was total darkness inside. Johnny knew his way around the cabin and made his way to the big table and lit his lantern. The light from his lantern created a dismal atmosphere. Flickering light from the lantern danced across the walls and black shadows hung in all corners of the cabin. In total exhaustion, Quenlyn sank to the floor. If she didn't get out of these wet clothes she would die of hypothermia.

Johnny move to the fire place, stacked logs on the dead coals and pored about a half pint of kerosene over the logs. Immediately, flames lit the room and danced eerily among the shadows.

Johnny grabbed Quenlyn's arms and dragged her close to the fire and then told her that she should take her clothes off and wrap herself up in a blanket he threw down on the floor beside her. At his suggestion she still did not move. She felt the warmth of the fire on her face and she passed out. Much later she awoke, a blanket had been wrapped around her and for the first time in 2 days, she felt warm. The fire had calmed down, but was providing warmth throughout the small log cabin. As morning crept over the mountains, it brought fog and more snow. With only two small windows, the light barely penetrated the cabin.

Johnny had not heard the dogs bark now for several hours and was delusional in thinking they would just give up and go away. He was hungry, but made no effort to eat. Neither did he think to feed his captives. He got out his double barrel shotgun and deer rifle and leaned them against the wall near the window that faced the creek. He had never been this nervous in his life.

****

A tracker friend of Mose's had shown up to take care of the dogs.

Everyone, including the Sheriff, had been up over twenty-four hours. Sheriff Dill suggested, "Let's get in our cars and warm up for an hour. Get some shut eye and then we'll see if we can formulate the next steps. Right now, I have an idea where to go from here."

****

Quenlyn had not moved, fearing her abductor. She knew he was somewhere in the room, but she did not dare give him any indication that she was awake. She touched her lips with her tongue and realized they were cracked and bleeding. She was very warm wrapped up in the quilt, but something was different. Then she realized that her hands were no longer tied behind her back, and she was naked under the blanket. This monster had undressed her when she was passed out. She slid her hand up her side and realized that he had also removed her underwear. Her worst fear was not that he might rape her, but that he would kill her afterwards.

In her peripheral vision, she saw that he had put something against the wall. He was not moving around in the room and she suspected that he may be sleeping. She was curious why he had untied her hands. The only sound was the crackling of the fire. Occasionally, she could hear the wind gust through the trees outside. There was a cold draft coming from the back window when the wind whipped up. Johnny had still not noticed the broken window.

Her sense of hearing had become acute in this tense situation. It was so quiet she could hear her own breathing. So when a low moaning sounded close to her, she shook in reaction to it. Was that her captor, sleeping on the floor next to her? Oh, God, she hoped not. She risked turning her head ever so slightly to the left, and saw a mound under a blanket. She looked harder and could see a chain leading from somewhere out of her view, to under the blanket. This had to be someone chained and held prisoner just like her. But why were they chained and she was not?

****

An hour later, the Sheriff roused the sleeping deputies and told them to get up and gather near the fire. Once everyone was out of their trucks, he told them what he had been thinking.

"I suspect that the man we are looking for is not out of this area. I don't know how he fooled the dogs, but I really do believe he is not far away. What I want us to do is fan out within a half mile of where we are and see if there is something we missed in the dark. Keep your walkee's on vibrate and report back to me if you see anything. No one is to engage this man on your own because most likely he is armed. Is that clear?"

Every man shook his head.

"OK, let's go in pairs and don't try to be a hero."

One of the deputies asked about the dogs.

"Sheriff, why are we not going to use the dogs to locate them?"

"Because I want that man to think that we have given up trying to find Ms. Maguire's scent. The dogs would make too much noise and we might not find her alive."

There were five men, not including the Sheriff, headed out in various directions. JC had a hunch that the man they were looking for was somewhere down along Slaughter Creek where the under growth was very thick. So he asked Sam to take one side of the creek and he would take the other.

"Stay close enough to see my hand signal if I need you to come to my side of the creek. Make sure you keep an outlook for any new footprints in the snow.

****

In the light of the morning, JC had found a place where he could step across the creek and back without getting his feet wet. Once on the other side he began to walk down the creek. He could easily see Sam's blue rain suit, on the opposite side of the creek. He was headed in the same direction as JC. It was quiet this morning and the snow seemed to be letting up. A solitary flock of crows could be heard as they made their morning rounds in search of something to eat.

The snow accumulation hit between eight and ten inches overnight. In this area, the lumber company had agreed to leave many of the virgin yellow popular trees and many topped over a hundred feet high. They were large in girth and a man could easily hide behind one. JC kept this in mind as he walked among them. These tall trees blocked out the sun limiting normal under growth. Only the mountain laurel and large rhododendron thrived under these giant trees.

This morning, JC could hear the crunch of his boots in the snow. His eyes were like lasers trying to see what could not be seen. He knew if there were footprints from the night before, they would be covered by the early morning snow. As instructed by the Sheriff, he had his walkie-talkie on vibrate. If he had to use it, he would tuck it under his coat and speak in a whisper.

****

Johnny was running low on fire wood and needed to go outside where he had a sufficient supply, but that would have to wait.

After exchanging his wet bib overalls for some dry ones, he took a long swig of whisky to warm his insides. The young woman was now unconscious and if she didn't get the wet clothes off, she could die. This was not part of his plan. He decided he needed to undress her himself then wrap her in his warmest blanket. Johnny had never had a relationship with a woman and had certainly never seen one naked, except in occasional magazines.

First he took off the hiking boots and socks and sat them near the fireplace to dry. Then his hands began to shake as he pulled her blue rain pants off, revealing her wet long johns. This exposed her small, but shapely body and for some reason he felt the same stimulation he had with dead bodies. Then the rain coat came off by rotating her body from one side to the other. Under the rain coat was a heavy jacket that also needed to be unzipped and with some effort he got if off as well. Now she was lying there with only her wet underwear on. As he pulled off her long johns he noticed her intricate curves and crevices. Johnny was thinking about how different her body was from the headless body's he had experienced over the years. Her skin was snow white with dark pubic hair. The thoughts he had now ran contrary to his normal pattern and he found himself convulsing at the touch of her body. Still he was intrigued by what he saw. He knelt down on the floor and lightly ran his fingers over her breast. Then all of a sudden his mind flipped back to its normal urges and he rolled her naked body onto the blanket and covered her with it. In order to get her clothes off, he had been forced to cut the tape from her hands, but after seeing her small lifeless body, did not tie her up again. He felt she was of no threat. Now after the harrowing night, he fell onto his bed and drifted into a deep sleep.

****

About a half mile had been covered down the creek, when JC noticed what appeared to be a set of tracks in the snow. They lead out from the stream, but he was puzzled because they were looking for two people.

JC signaled to Sam, indicating he had found something and motioned for Sam to wait for further instructions. The possibility that he had stumbled across the man they were looking for sent a shot of adrenalin through him. As a ranger, he had never even pulled his pistol out of its holster. If ever there was a time, it was now. Not wanting to destroy the tracks, he walked to the side of them and headed towards a very dense rhododendron thicket. He had second thoughts about going into the thicket alone and returned to the spot where he could see Sam waiting. He motioned for Sam to cross the stream and join him.

"Look over here," JC whispered. "I found one set of prints that appear to be headed into that rhododendron thicket. I'm not comfortable going in alone, so I want you to follow me at a safe distance. Keep in sight and watch for my hand signals. If we see something suspicious, I'll let the Sheriff know where we are and we can wait for backup."

Sam did not have a gun nor was he trained for this kind of work. But this was his cousin and he knew that he'd assist in any way he could.

****

Johnny had been awake for some time and even though he had not heard the hounds for several hours he remained edgy. He was cautious, but thought his ruse just might have worked. He was hungry, but couldn't risk firing up his Colman stove fearing that the smell of cooking food might bring the dogs back. Instead, he put some peanut butter and jelly on several slices of stale bread. He knew Chandler had not had anything to eat since yesterday so he put two slices on a tin plate and laid it on the floor and filled a glass up with water. Even thought he had removed the tape off the man's mouth, he had not uttered a word. He kicked the man a little and told him to wake up, that he had company.

Quenlyn laying there within arm's reach of Chandler watched this exchange. Then Johnny leaned down and said, "Here's something for you to pretty girl with the golden hair." How was she going to eat this horrible food with duct tape over her mouth? It was at that moment that she realized how befuddled her mind was. Her hands were free and she could reach up and take the tape off herself.

"Go ahead, take it off. I don't care. I ain't heard a voice in days."

For the first time Quenlyn dared to rise up on one elbow and pull the tape off her mouth. She stole a quick glance at the man. He looked like somebody out of a monster movie. She really didn't want to eat the bread, but decided it was best to patronize him, fearing he could become violent. Her arms were inside the blanket so she had to slip one out in order to pick the bread up. Johnny just remained in a crouch position watching her and grinning.

Chandler's condition had worsened. He moved in and out of consciousness and knew that if his situation did not change soon, he would not survive. He had a sense that someone lay close to him but could not muster the strength to roll over.

Quenlyn knew that Johnny was staring at her from his crouched position. She chose to not make eye contact, but also made no movement to indicate she was unsettled by his attention. She just took a bite of the bread and chewed on it slowly so that it dissolved in her mouth. Had she known that the buckets lining the front wall held seven well preserved human heads, she couldn't have finished the bread. Fortunately for her, Johnny had not felt the need to display the grotesque heads as he had to Chandler.

While he was down on his haunches, she noticed a sudden change in his eyes. His eyes had been focused on her, then suddenly they closed up and he squinted like he was trying to listen. Quenlyn had not heard anything unusual, but Johnny had. He quietly rose and made a slow turn heading to the front window that faced the creek. Gently, he pulled one of the ragged window curtains aside and peeked out. He saw nothing. Then he walked quietly to the front door and put his ear to it, listened intently. Still he did not hear anything. There was something out there. He was convinced of it...maybe a deer looking for something to eat. The snow was heavy throughout the mountains and it was not all that uncommon for animals to search out trash cans for food. But Johnny did not have a trash can. The sound he thought he had heard was a very faint metallic noise. The only metal outside the cabin were the two 55 gallon drums against the back of the side wall, which he could not see from either window.

Quenlyn decided that this man must be a fugitive from the law and he was afraid that they might be near. But she had not heard the dogs for some time and wondered if they had given up on finding her. She prayed that her rescuers were near and that they would find her before this man decided to do something awful. The irony was that Johnny was not a fugitive because the law did not have any reason to look for him. They were looking for her and the young man beside her on the floor.

****

The forecast was calling for more snow that day at higher elevations keeping the temperatures low. More wood was needed inside the cabin, but at the moment, Johnny was on high alert and wood was not his priority. He would wait for a while before going outside to get fire wood. First he wanted to satisfy himself that there was not someone waiting for him outside.

JC, with his pistol drawn, followed the zig zag path through the old growth of rhododendron. The snow on the leaves above created an overhead shroud. JC continued at a slow pace and soon a very old log cabin came into view. Half the roof was covered with a black tarp. He could smell smoke in the area, but did not see any coming from the chimney. From where he stood, he thought he was out of sight of the window. The tracks he had been following led right to the door. This had to be who they were searching for and yet there was no car, no road to the cabin and no mailbox.

Wanting to stay out of sight, he decided to take a long route back to the right end of the cabin where he could make his approach unseen. Before doing this, he went back to Sam and told him the plan. Sam could not yet see the cabin, so JC told him to move in closer until he could see it in case he was needed, but to stay out of sight.

JC walked about a hundred yards below the cabin before he made a U-turn and came back up on the windowless chimney side of the cabin. He was thinking that maybe he should have already called the Sheriff for back up, but since he was in place, he would go ahead and check the back side of the cabin first. He wanted to see if there was a back door. He crept towards the cabin with caution, fully aware that someone could burst through the door with a gun.

Upon approaching the cabin form its blind side, JC was puzzled by the two rusty steel drums sitting next to the cabins outside wall. Maybe they were being used to hold water, but that would be highly unlikely because there was plenty of water in the stream near the cabin. Once he was up against the building he made his move to peek around the corner to see if there was a backdoor. He was relieved to see that there was no back door, so he moved back to chimney. While he was standing there pondering what his next move should be, he could see that someone had padlocked each barrel. What on earth could be worth protecting at this place?

One lock looked like it was set in place but not totally snapped. JC could not resist lifting the lid just slightly to see what was so valuable. He cautiously removed the lock from its latch, careful not to make a sound. To lift the lid, he had to wipe off about six inches of snow. He gently pried his fingers under the lid and slowly raised it about ten inches before peering in. At first it looked like tannic acid water. It was a clear fluid, but definitely had a rusty tint. It was then that a horrible stench hit him in the face. He was about to close the lid when he saw something that turned his stomach.

Just under the surface of the fluid, he could make out what appeared to be human fingers reaching upwards. JC gasped and almost choked at the discovery and unintentionally let the lid drop back into place. It was that noise that Johnny had heard on the inside of the cabin.

JC now realized that he had gone well beyond his capabilities. He knew that he should have alerted the Sheriff when he had discovered the tracks leading to the cabin. Now the possibility of being discovered by whoever was inside could very well become a reality.

****

JC crept back into the woods and called the sheriff. A crackling noise on the walkie-talkie alerted Sheriff Dill that one of the men was trying to reach him.

"Sheriff, JC here," whispered JC into his radio.

"You got me, go ahead"

"Sheriff, Sam and I have found a cabin a couple of hundred yards off the road and across the creek. I discovered footprints in the snow which led me to the cabin."

"I'm almost certain the man we are looking for is in that cabin and probably the two young people as well. I found evidence that will turn your stomach and I think we have a very dangerous killer on our hands. I will have Sam Hardgrave meet you at the road to show you where I'm hidden next to the cabin. This could develop into a hostage situation, so exercise extreme caution."

"We'll be there ASAP," replied Sheriff Dill.

The Sheriff immediately contacted dispatch and ordered four more deputies to high tail it to the Slaughter Gap Road.

JC motioned to Sam that he should go back to the road and wait for their backup.

****

There had not been anymore sounds outside, but Johnny was not convinced that he had imagined that noise. Someone or something could be just out of sight on the blind side of the cabin. Quenlyn watched him as he stepped over to the door and picked up his deer rifle. He slipped and extra clip of ammo in his pocket and again carefully looked out the front window. The shadows of the rhododendrons prevented him from seeing very far into the thicket. There was no movement so he crossed the room to the back window. When he pulled back the curtain, he discovered the broken window. This came as a total surprise and he blurted out, "How the Hell did this happen?" Chandler had known that Johnny would discover the window sooner or later. Despite his semiconscious state, he knew enough to expect the worst.

At first it did not register with Johnny that the window had been broken from the inside. The possibility of someone finding his cabin had his complete attention. Unconsciously, he used the broken window to his advantage, sticking his rifle out of the hole. At that very moment, JC was looking around the corner of the cabin, and caught the movement. He now knew for certain they had a hostage situation on their hands.

****

With two deputies and a park ranger in tow, the sheriff headed down the road until they saw Sam. Sam reported to Dill about what he had seen from the thicket. He relayed that there was only one small window and a door on the front side of the cabin.

JC dialed his walkie-talkie volume as low as he could get it, but he still heard the click that signaled a message from the Sheriff.

"JC, we are out here and can see the cabin. I have five men with me, including Sam. From your vantage point, at the back, what do you suggest?"

JC whispered into his radio. "Have the two men most experienced in these woods work their way around to the opposite end of the cabin from where I'm located. There are only two windows, so you won't be seen, but silence will be key. One window is on the front and the other is on the back near me.

"Someone in the cabin is armed with a long gun. My guess is he'll be willing to use it. The door may be secured and if we attempt to force our way in, it could prove to be tragic for the people he is holding."

JC continued. "I believe he suspects someone is outside. A rifle poked through a hole in the back window just before I called you. What do you think of getting his attention with a bull horn?"

Dill had been the Sheriff of Union County now for over twenty years. With thousands of square miles and only a handful of deputies, he had never run into a hostage situation. He had called for more backup, but it would take precious time and he did not believe he had that luxury. If you corner a bear, the chances are the bear is going to feel the need to fight. This was the way he sized up the situation.

"I agree JC. I think our first option is to reason with him. We'll take it from there, depending on how he reacts. There is only one entrance into the cabin so we can't risk ramming the door. If he is holding the Maguire woman and the Chandler boy hostage, he could get desperate and kill them. I'm going to call out and see if he will respond, so be ready."

Dill did not have a bull horn, but for this situation his loud, deep voice would be an asset. He positioned himself near the opposite end of the cabin from JC.

Chapter 29
Jeopardy

Nearly an hour had passed since Johnny thought he heard a noise outside. He could see no movement from either window, no hounds were baying and there were no more unusual metallic sounds. So, he decided that his imagination had played tricks on him. He'd been through a lot the night before and it wouldn't be the first time he had imagined hearing noises.

Until now Quenlyn had not dared speak to the man who had taken her captive, but he had spoken to her this morning and his manner had not been threatening. Still, he had not returned her clothes and she felt very vulnerable with only the dirty blanket wrapped around her. So mustering courage, she looked Johnny in the eye and asked,

"Could I please have my clothes back? There's no fire and I'm cold."

Johnny opened his mouth to respond when all of a sudden, the silence was broken a the deep voice from just outside the cabin.

Johnny froze as a chill shot up his spine. The voice was calling to him.

"Sir, I'm the Union County Sheriff and I would like you to open your window or door so that we can talk."

Johnny's reclusive inclinations created fear and suspicion. At this point in his life, he trusted no one...except maybe his sister. This situation paralyzed him and he possessed no ability to respond under stress. Quenlyn, who had started to sit up, now quickly lay back down and pulled the blanket tightly around her. If there was ever a chance to escape this madman, this may be it. She was not bound by a rope or duct tape any longer and her adrenalin was elevated by hearing the Sheriff's voice.

Still confused, the only thing Johnny knew was to keep a strong grip on his gun. But his hands began to tremble. Being totally unprepared to deal with the law, his instinct was to kill. However, this time his mind would not provide him the clarity to act. Although he had killed many times, he was a coward. In all those deaths he had never faced those whose throats he had cut. He had always taken pleasure in seeing his victims bleed, but the sight of his own blood was repulsive. Somewhere in

185

that confused psyche, Johnny knew this time he was the victim and suddenly he did not want to die.

Receiving no response, the Sheriff called out again.

"Sir, can you hear me? We need to talk. I don't want anyone to get hurt, so please open your door just wide enough for you and I to speak."

Johnny could hear every word the man said, but remained silent. The Sheriff was becoming impatient, so he did not wait long before calling out again.

"Sir, you might not want to talk to me, but understand, your cabin is surrounded and we don't plan to leave. We have reason to believe that you are holding two hostages. You need to let them walk out of the door unharmed. If you do, no harm will come to you. Let's resolve this peacefully without anyone getting hurt. Can you hear me?"

Inside the cabin, Quenlyn noticed a drool was running down the corners of Johnny's mouth. It was all she could do not to vomit, watching the unsightly saliva rolling through his beard and dripping on the floor. Johnny's stomach was tormenting him and his headache of last night was back with a vengeance. This must be what a trapped cougar feels like, he thought.

Quenlyn decided she might help break the stalemate and softly suggested, "Why don't you talk to him? Maybe he'll go away."

Johnny turned and screamed at her, "Shut up bitch. You say or do anything and I'll cut your pretty head right off." With that he pulled out the big knife and pointed it at her. It was a good thing she was not aware that it had been used for that very purpose many times before.

Sheriff Dill could hear Johnny's threats through the drafty cabin walls. He decided this was looking more like the cornered bear situation so he remained quiet for a while to see if the tense moment would pass. The Sheriff knew that pushing too hard was not wise. It was paramount that he get the safe release of those two young people. How he was going to accomplish this, he had no clue.

It was Johnny that made the next move. He could not raise the window, so he unlocked the door and opened it just a few inches. He didn't stand in the open as he didn't want to give the Sheriff a clear shot. Putting his mouth near the barely opened door, he spoke for the first time.

"What ya want?"

Dill recognized this as a break in his favor.

"We just want you to let the two young people go. Nobody needs to get hurt. You are in control. I promise that we will not hurt you. Just lay down your gun and come out. There will be no guns pointed at you. We just need to talk."

This was again met with total silence. Dill stuck his head around the corner and could see the end of Johnny's rifle pointing out the door. Dill knew he had a very dangerous situation on his hands. He again pushed for a dialog.

"Sir, I know you don't want to get hurt. Please for the sake of everyone, let's do the right thing."

Somewhere in Johnny's head he knew he should not give up that easily so he shoved the door closed and locked it. He looked over at Quenlyn and told her to get up and to come over to him. Fear ripped through her, but she had no choice. Was he going to kill her or would he use them as pawns to gain his freedom?

Quenlyn slowly got to her feet holding the blanket tightly around her body with both arms.

She walked the few steps nearer, but just out of reach to where Johnny was standing.

He knew what she was doing and screamed, "Get over here bitch!"

He didn't wait for her to move, but reached over and grabbed her long hair pulling her head backwards. He held her head at an angle that only allowed her see the ceiling. She gasped, but found it difficult to breathe. He was pulling on her so hard, that she feared she'd fall over. He leaned the rifle next to the door, and again pulled the big knife from his belt and kicked the door open. He couldn't see anyone, so in a loud gravelly voice he told the Sheriff to show himself. In that instant, he placed the knife blade under Quenlyn's chin. She closed her eyes and prayed that it would be quick.

Sheriff Dill moved out from the corner of the cabin, but remained at a safe distance. He had no gun in his hand. What Johnny didn't see was another deputy behind a tree with a bead right between Johnny's eyes. Dill knew that the next few moments would mean life of death for Quenlyn. He raised his hands above his head and turned around slowly, to show Johnny that he was not armed.

"What is you want sir?" asked Dill.

"I wants yo and yo other lawmen to all show yo self in front of me and I mean the one I know is at the end of my cabin. Den I wants ya to all lay yo guns down in front of me where I ken see 'em."

"If we agree to do what you're asking, are you going to shoot us?" Dill was curious about how this crazy man might respond.

"No, I gonna ask all of yo to walk one behind the other towards dat creek. Then I'll let this girl go."

"Do we have your word on that?" Dill asked knowing that he had the advantage of the deputy still hidden with the bead drawn on Johnny's forehead.

"I will let her go. I give my word on dat and I won't shoot youse all in da back."

There was no way to know if this man would do as he promised, but right now, the situation was precarious. He had a knife to the woman's throat.

"All RIGHT YOU MEN, come out and do like this man says. Put your guns out here where he can watch you do it and then head back towards the creek"

Johnny felt ecstatic. He had no idea he could wield so much power over lawmen. He watched as each of them laid down their weapon in the snow and began walking towards the creek. Dill had no idea if Johnny would take the woman back into the cabin or out into the woods as his hostage. Once beyond the vision of the cabin, Dill lay down in the snow-covered thicket and watched the cabin door. If Johnny did move away from the cabin they stood a better chance to nail him.

****

Quenlyn knew in her heart that this man would cut her throat. But that did not happen. She was surprised when Johnny pulled her back into the cabin and gave her a hard push onto the floor. Without the burden of the woman, he could out run and out maneuver any of them. He put on his coat, grabbed some jerky and his rifle. He flew out the door and headed around the cabin to the west. His cabin stood nestled at the foot of Blood Mountain. The deputy hiding behind the tree took a shot but missed, as Johnny disappeared behind the cabin.

Quenlyn was quick. Her father had taught her to shoot at an early age and she was a natural with a gun. In his rush to get away, Johnny had overlooked the loaded 12 gage shot gun leaning against the wall.

She jumped up, grabbed the gun with the hand that was not holding the blanket and ran to the back window. There she saw Johnny scampering up the bank trying to make his escape. She forgot the blanket and pointed the double barrel gun at Johnny through the broken window. She did not want to kill him so she took careful aim his legs. She pulled the trigger one shot right after another. With a loud explosion and the accompanying smoke, Johnny went down.

Chapter 30
The Aftermath

The echo of the shotgun's double barrel explosion boomeranged off the mountain and down into the valley. The Sheriff and his team came running back to the cabin. They peered in to see if the Maguire lady was ok, dreading that they might find her with her throat cut, and at the same time wondering who had fired the shotgun.

What they found was a naked young woman armed with a smoking shotgun. As she realized the condition of her clothing, she quickly grabbed the blanket to cover herself. Two deputies ran to the back of the cabin and found the wounded man lying face down on the ground. The rifle he was carrying had flown twelve feet when he was hit. With all guns pointing at him they still approached him with caution. They could see that the shotgun blasts at close range had struck him in the back of his legs and he was bleeding profusely. First they handcuffed him and then used their belts as tourniquets above his knees to stop the bleeding.

Back in the cabin, the Sheriff cleared his throat discreetly. "I assume you are Quenlyn Maguire?" When she nodded, he continued. "You o.k?"

She turned around and saw the red faces of the deputies. Indigently she responded, "I'm fine! I'm just incredibly tired and I want to go home. But first this young man lying on the floor needs emergency help ASAP." Dill jerked his head toward a deputy in non-verbal direction to call 911.

Quenlyn actually felt like she was going to collapse from exhaustion and hunger. She continued, "I have had almost nothing to eat since Friday, and I'm afraid this guy may have gone many more days without much food."

Dill took one look at Chandler and told one of his deputies to call and request two EMS teams.

Quenlyn asked the men to give her a few moments of privacy. She desperately wanted to get her clothes back on.

****

With Johnny in custody, JC grabbed the Sheriff by the arm. "Sheriff, I have something outside you have to see."

The two walked around to the chimney side of the cabin. "This will make you sick!" warned JC.

This time, JC lifted the lid completely off and stepped back. The over-powering stench hit the Sheriff in the face, just as it had JC earlier. Dill was so repulsed, that he took two steps back and puked.

"My God, what's in there?" JC responded that he thought the smell was formaldehyde, usually used for preserving specimens in a lab. "In this case," JC continued, "I think the drum holds human remains. Put something over your nose and mouth so you can step closer. Look at what is just under the surface."

The Sheriff did as JC directed.

"OH GOD! What have we discovered?"

"I'm betting," JC continued, "there is a corpse attached to the hand we're looking at and I'll put down money that the other barrel contains similar human remains."

Dill mumbled through his handkerchief, "Not that I really want to, but we better take a look."

JC found a hammer in the cabin and knocked the lock off the other barrel. He lifted the lid and took a cautious look. In this barrel, nothing was easily visible at the top, so JC picked up a stick and poked around in the fluid.

"There is definitely something down there, but I suggest we wait and let the forensics team make the discovery." Dill was more than happy for the forensics guys to enjoy that experience.

****

It took an hour for the two EMS trucks to arrive from Bristol. The snow and the remoteness of the road had made it difficult for them to find Slaughter Cap. Once Sam could get in the cabin, he rushed to Quenlyn to see if she was o.k. Quenlyn was not happy about all the fuss and assured him that she would be fine. All she wanted was a shower, 12 hours of sleep and a couple of hot meals.

Feeling comfortable that his cousin would be fine, he volunteered to direct the EMS crews to the cabin.

One team was directed to give Johnny medical attention, while the other team headed into the cabin to get Chandler on a stretcher. Quenlyn insisted that she could walk to the cars. She adamantly refused to ride in an ambulance.

When Chandler was lifted onto the stretcher, he regained consciousness just long enough to point to the five-gallon buckets against the inside cabin wall. "Heads," he croaked. "Look inside the cans."

After Chandler was out of the cabin, Sheriff Dill, now a little skittish about covered barrels, walked over to the containers. He truly hoped this would not prove to be more putrefied body parts. The cabin was very dark. The only light came from the open door. As his eyes adjusted, he recognized what he was seeing. He was repulsed for the second time. This time, staring back at him were the eyes of Johnny's only friend, Jay Goddard. "Oh God!" he uttered again. Dill counted five buckets. He could not bring himself to open them all, but peered into just one more to confirm his suspicions. No questions now about Johnny being a serial killer. In danger of puking a second time, Dill tore out of the cabin in great need for some fresh air. He immediately called his office in Bristol. This was far beyond his pay grade!

Before he could say anything to his assistant Anne, she blurted out, "Did you catch the guy? Did you find the two hikers?"

"Yes, Anne we did", Sheriff Dill informed her patiently. "Now listen to me very carefully. I want

197

you to call the Georgia State Police. I will meet them at the Suches Post Office. Tell them we have uncovered a serial killer. There are at least two corpses and a number of severed human heads at this location. We need the forensics up here ASAP." With that news he hung up before Anne could ask any more questions.

Quenlyn had walked out to the road unassisted where Sam and Hawk were waiting. Hawk had come down from the Woods Hole Shelter and was delighted to see Quenlyn. Tears prickled in all three cousins eyes as they clung to each other for a long time.

Finally, the Sheriff had good news to report. Both Quenlyn's and Robert Chandler's parents were waiting at a motel near Suches. He assured Quenlyn's parents that she was fine and would be delivered to them by a deputy. Chandler's parents headed to the hospital.

The Sheriff told the cousins, "You can head to the motel, but I need the three of you stay overnight so we can piece this together in the morning. Given the severity of what we found, the FBI will want to talk with you as well. Ms. Maguire, are you sure you don't need to go to the hospital?"

"No Sir," Quenlyn replied. All I need now is a good glass of wine, a hot meal and 12 hours of undisturbed sleep. Don't worry. I'll be OK." Underneath her brave and confidant sounding voice, she was still trembling. Later that evening, while the law enforcement was investigating the crime scene at the foot of Blood Mountain, the entire Maquire family was celebrating Quenlyn's safe return over the hot meal she had requested. The Chandlers were headed to the Bristol Hospital to be with their son, Robert.

Johnny Greene was also taken to the Bristol Hospital for surgery where he would be kept under heavy guard and then transferred to a Federal prison near Atlanta. The injuries Quenlyn had inflicted on him, meant he would never walk again without the aid of crutches.

Greene would give a full confession and after only a year, he was brought to trial in Federal Court. In 1973, prior to his trial, the Georgia Legislature would reinstate the death penalty. DNA from the corpses found in the two barrels, was traced back to hikers reported missing several years before. DNA from four of the heads found in the cabin would match four migrant workers, killed and beheaded in Florida. As far as Jay Goddard was concerned, because he had never been arrested, no DNA match was available and the fifth head would never be identified. The state of Florida would try to have him extradited to stand trial for the four migrant workers, but this was rejected by Georgia who wanted to make sure Greene would be executed.

Near the end of Greene's confession, he was asked about a human arm bone that was found in the fireplace in the Blood Mountain Shelter. With nothing to lose, he boasted that he had left the arm bone in the ashes after spending one night in the shelter. He claimed to have cut it off one of the people he had killed on the Appalachian Trail. He had preserved it in vinegar for about a year and then roasted and ate it only the week before he was captured. This was the bone that Hawk had discovered the first night in the Blood Mountain Shelter fireplace the night of February 15th 1973.

Chandler, Hawk, Sam and Quenlyn were all called to testify at Greene's trial. When asked to identify her abductor, Quenlyn looked straight into Johnny Greene's eyes, pointed at him and said, "That's the bastard sitting right in that chair."

Greene was convicted of seven murders in all and was put on death row. Seven years later, on February 16th 1980 with shackles on his hands and ankles, Green shuffled down halls of the Georgia maximum security prison for the final time. A rope was placed around his neck and the platform beneath his feet dropped out from underneath him. He hung there, swinging from the rope until all the blood had drained from his face and he was declared dead. The only one present at the hanging was an elderly woman named Elsey.

The End

About the author

L arry Greer had always dreamed of being a through-hiker on the Appalachian Trail, which runs 2,200 miles from Springer Mountain, Georgia to Mt Katahdin, Maine. However, because of his wife's illness, he opted for multiple short hikes over the course of several decades. To date, he has hiked the Smokey Mountain National Park 28 times, racking up 1,932 miles on the AT!

In 1972, along with two of his cousins, they hiked the portion of the Appalachian Trail about which this book is written. They stayed in the Blood Mountain Shelter one night, which inspired this story.

Made in the USA
San Bernardino, CA
11 June 2019